THE SUITE

TEA SOCIETY

The Boss Moves Series

TINA LUCKETT

For more information on the author,
please visit her website:

www.TinaLuckett.com

Executive Chief Art Designer: Lanier Burton, Coolesdolo
Cover Design: Jami L West, JLWestDesign
Editing: Virginia Cantrell, Barbara Hoover, Hot Tree Editing
Beta Readers: Kyra Zirlin, Diana Ginard, Hot Tree Editing Proofreading:
Robert Martin, Hot Tree Editing
Formatting: Polgarus Studio

Library of Congress Control Number: 2022905836

ISBN: 979-8-4490258-7-6 - PAPERBACK
ISBN: 979-8-8009038-4-3 - HARDBACK
ISBN: 978-1-7364090-0-8 - EBOOK

For my family, I love you all.

CONTENTS

ACKNOWLEDGEMENTS

For my loving husband, Lawrence "Larry" Luckett, I know I kept you in the dark for most of the book but trust me, it's worth the wait.

To my hardworking and amazing daughters, Breanna Luckett-Jackson and Areanna Luckett, I am blessed to have you in my life; it would be empty without you. To my son-in-law, Lazarus Jackson, thanks for finding my daughter; you two have given me the best joy in the world, my grandson, Chance Jackson. Jamal Daramy, thanks for being there when Areanna needed you.

To my mom, Leah Felicia Myles, what can I say? I love you to the moon and back. Thanks for our daily calls.

To my dad, Jimmy "James" Watson, thank you for raising me to be the lady I am today. All of those hard stares did work; look at me, I'm a published author, and my stepmother, Patricia, thanks for being there for my dad.

I couldn't have written this book if it wasn't for my sisters, Carolyn "Cat" Watson, Chantelle Harris, Tiah Harris, Keywonder Curtis, Yvonne Wilson, and Ulonda Forest; I love you all.

My sister Cat and her son Lanier Burton were there when I needed a push. If they didn't push me, this book would still be sitting in my files on my laptop. Thank you both so much; I needed that push.

I'm forever indebted to all my aunts, cousins, friends, and co-workers; it's just too many to name at this time; thanks for listening to me brag about this book.

Special thanks to:

Antoinette Davis, thanks for being my best friend for all of these years. I love our Sunday's talks.

Lisha Lewis, I couldn't have written this book if it wasn't for the support I received from you everyday.

Patrice Smith, thanks for having my back since high school.

Christy Debrezeny, you asked me each week, "When will I let the world meet Trina." Well, Christy, right now. Thanks for keeping Trina relevant.

Donna Lehman, thanks for adding your suggestions. This book is a lot better now.

ACT 1

TRINA'S REVENGE

CHAPTER 1

DANIELLE

B reakfast was quiet, as it always was.

"I'm going on a business trip today. I'll be back in a week," Brad O'Connell said, his eyes on the morning paper.

Danielle took a sip of tea and rested the teacup on the saucer. She wasn't surprised about the sudden announcement from her husband. Brad was a busy man, and he had to travel without much notice several times throughout the month. She only wished that he would have given her more notice this time. They had planned to meet with his mother and sister for lunch later today.

"Your mother and sister will be disappointed that you aren't joining us for lunch," Danielle said.

Brad shrugged. "I'm sure you'll keep them company, won't you, Danielle? You're a great host." He graced her with a smile before returning his attention back to his paper.

Being a great host had nothing to do with her wanting him to be there for lunch. His sister and mother could be quite overwhelming. Most times, they acted like she wasn't there. And they always had one complaint after another. She couldn't help but wonder if they talked about her that way in her absence And, of course, Brad would never own up to any of their pettiness.

A knock on the door announced Timothy's arrival. Brad's loyal driver was a small man who always dressed in dark clothes—or at least he had for as long as Danielle had known him. He nodded in greeting and picked up the black luggage near the door that Danielle hadn't even noticed.

Brad glanced at his watch and got up on cue. "Do you need anything?"

"I will need some money while you're gone," Danielle said.

"Talk to Sally," he said, referring to his accountant. He patted her on the shoulder, and she watched her husband leave. Not even a kiss goodbye.

She had a lot she wanted to talk to him about. Where was he going? Which client was he meeting? But those were questions she wasn't supposed to ask, and she was concerned.

Eight years earlier, while attending her parents' Christmas party, Danielle met Brad. It was love at first sight for her, but not so for him. Over the years and after a little push from their parents to get married, Danielle married Brad when she was twenty-two years old.

Some might call Danielle's life perfect because she didn't have to work, and her days were spent socializing and attending to the duties of the charity she ran with some of the other wealthy housewives. The latter gave her fulfillment, and she put hours into it, making use of her human psychology degree.

The huge house had been a wedding gift from their parents. It was in a gated estate filled with impressive homes. Danielle loved keeping up her home and organizing parties. Her husband met her financial needs, who was the CEO of her parents' company. She could run the business, but why should she? He provided everything she needed, and she didn't have to worry about anything. Plus, Brad liked being in charge.

Danielle left the house for her lunch with her in-laws. She was dressed in a brown dress, her brown hair pulled into a neat ponytail, and she'd accessorized with pearls she had inherited from her grandmother and a pair of dark sunglasses for the scorching sun.

Pierre was a family-owned, five-star restaurant in Bloomfield Hills—a small city in the northern suburb of Metro Detroit in Michigan. The food was decent, but it was where everyone wanted to be seen. The décor was great, but it had lots of open windows and doors, which was fantastic in the summer.

She found Brad's mother and sister on the patio—their usual spot. Martha was in her late fifties, but she looked a lot younger, courtesy of her surgeons. She was small of stature, which she had kept trim over the years. Cindy was a gorgeous model. She was skinny with long legs, which went with her line of business. She had no problem demanding attention when she walked into a room. Her only downfall was her lousy attitude.

"You have added a few pounds," Cindy sneered before taking a long sip from her glass of lemonade.

Danielle nodded. She knew it hadn't been her imagination. She did need to start working out. Just that morning, she'd found it difficult getting into her dress. This meant she would have to resume Pilates.

Martha removed her sunglasses and peered behind her. "Where's Brad?"

"He went on a work trip today. He won't be back for a week. He sends his apologies," Danielle said.

"Hmmpphh. Didn't he go on a trip two weeks ago? He's been going on trips more often," Martha said.

"Yes, he has a lot of work."

"Indeed." Cindy exchanged a look with her mother.

Danielle pretended not to notice, so she blew it off. She knew they only showed up to see Brad.

She would love to have her husband around more often. He had been present during the early years of their marriage, but as the company expanded, he spent more and more time in the office, leaving early in the morning and returning late at night. At times, he even returned the next day. She wished there was a way she could help, but the few times she had suggested sharing in the management, he had told her he would handle the burden.

The lunch lasted for an hour, which was long enough for Danielle. Anything longer than that would have been pure torture. She returned to the big, quiet house. They had a small staff that grew larger when parties were thrown. It was something she had been raised with. She didn't mingle with the staff; they were there to do the work they were paid for and nothing more.

She checked her calendar for the coming days. There was a charity ball tomorrow, which she did not want to attend. Who had a charity event on a Wednesday afternoon? However, the hosts were friends of their parents, and Brad had given a donation on their behalf. She wished he was home so they could go together. Lately, she had been going to events alone and had to give one explanation or another for her husband's absence while adding that he worked too much.

The day after the charity ball, she was free of any appointments, which meant she could fit in a day at the spa. She dialed her favorite spa, St. Anne Beauties. It was owned by a renowned plastic surgeon, whom she was considering using for some procedures if Brad agreed to them. They had an opening, and she was booked.

She sighed and checked the time. She still had a long way to go before going to bed. Despite the glam, her life was dull. She had a few friends, but they were usually occupied with family, work, or charity. Some of them took delight in shopping. While she had a shopping allowance, it wasn't an activity she was crazy about; she only did it when necessary.

Danielle hated spending her days like this—empty. She needed to find some activities to make her days more enjoyable. If only they had children, she thought with sadness.

Eight years in, she wasn't a mother like she had hoped to be. It was not from lack of trying on her part. She and Brad used to have a healthy sex life. Years ago, she had convinced him to do some tests, and the results showed nothing was wrong with either of them. Most of her friends were mothers to two or more children, and she always felt an emptiness and even jealousy when she saw them with their bundles of joy. They would tell her she was lucky that she didn't have to deal with the mess of children, even when they had a ton of nannies. But that mess was what she wanted—to have children fill the house with laughter.

The times she had talked to Brad about having children, he had dismissed the idea. It seemed being childless didn't bother him, but it did bother her. He would say they didn't need brats right now, and they were great together, but she needed a child she could dote on. She didn't want to be a nagging wife, but it seemed she would have to raise the discussion again.

Of the activities this week, the one she looked forward to most was attending the tea party. Two years ago, her neighbor Mrs. Aniston had invited her to a tea party before returning to London. It had been a surprise invitation because she had barely spoken with the other woman–Brad considered Mrs. Aniston an idiot with a loose mouth. But that didn't stop Mrs. Aniston from just showing up unannounced.

"You are coming to my tea party," she had said with a heavy accent.

Brad hadn't been home during that time either, so she'd decided to attend. A few days later, Danielle had gone to the tea party next door. It had turned out different from what she had expected. Her experience of tea parties was limited to the ones she had with her toy dolls when she was younger.

Danielle learned that this tea party was like no other. It didn't matter that it was a Sunday afternoon; these women drank whatever came their way. And tea wasn't on the menu. Vodka, wine, and a little tequila worked.

The tea party was a small circle of about fifteen women—some she knew from afar and some she didn't but had heard of in passing. She assumed they would talk about charities and politics, a way to develop and enlighten themselves. However, the major topic was fashion and, of course, gossip! In a way, it exceeded her expectation. On Sundays, she got to hear the major issues firsthand. Danielle often didn't participate in the conversations, but she listened, taking it all in. All the wives, like her, were married to wealth. Most times, they were housewives who had nothing to do but spend their day socializing. Perhaps to console their giving minds, they engaged in a charity cause a few times. At these parties, she felt some sort of kinship, even if she knew they would talk about her the moment she turned away.

In the two years since Danielle started going to the tea parties, she could count on her fingers how many times she had been absent. She had her favorite members and those she despised in their circle, but she would never show her feelings like the other women.

The days seemed to stretch on until Sunday, but she was waiting for what appeared to be the only fun activity in her rather dull life.

CHAPTER 2

GWEN

"You are an idiot!" Gwen Didier yelled at the waitress. She glared at the sorry excuse for a human being.

"I... am sorry—"

"Of course you are! Do you know how much this coat cost? More than you will ever make in a lifetime!"

"Gwen, it's okay. It was a mistake, and everyone's staring," Gwen's cousin Sophie said softly.

Gwen looked around to catch the eyes looking away. She scoffed. As if she cared. She was used to the attention. What she did care about was her Burberry coat.

She turned her attention back to the whimpering waitress. "Get me your manager!"

"Ma'am, I'm sorry. It was a mistake. I—"

"Do I look like a ma'am to you?" Gwen asked in a higher tone. She hated being called ma'am. That title was reserved for old, wrinkly grandmothers and not for her with her youth, beauty, and style.

"Why don't you go away? I'll handle this," Sophie told the waitress, who gratefully scurried off.

Gwen frowned at her companion. "Why did you do that? You know, you could have had my back."

"Gwen, it was a mistake; things happen. The poor girl was frightened."

"You know what? I will be in the car!" She shrugged out of her coat and dumped it on the table. It was a waste now. "Fucking stupid place!" she announced before texting her driver that she was done with this place. This was the last time she would come to this restaurant; she was going to make some calls and have it blacklisted by all her friends until an official apology was made.

Her black Cadillac pulled up in front of her. Grant, the driver, hurried out to fetch the door for her.

"Drive!" Gwen said as she settled into the leather seats.

"Will Ms. Sophie be joining us?"

Just as she was about to snap at him for asking such a dumb question, the door opened, and Sophie got in, taking deep breaths.

"You are lucky. I would have left you," Gwen sneered.

"I know… I know…."

The ride was tense, with Gwen fuming. Sophie irritated her most times. She should have had her back for once, but instead, Sophie felt sorry for the waitress.

"I'm sorry, Gwen, but the way you reacted was overwhelming. It was just a coat, and you can have it dry-cleaned or, better yet, purchase thousands more."

"First, it was not just a coat. That was a limited-edition Burberry. And you should have just kept quiet. Grant, drop her ass off at her place—I can't stand her anymore—then drive me home."

Gwen was supposed to spend the rest of the day with her cousin, but with her foul mood, she just couldn't deal.

"I'll call you," Sophie said when the car stopped in front of her townhouse.

Gwen ignored her, her eyes on her phone. However, she knew she would no longer be pissed off with her cousin by the end of the day.

"I've changed my mind. Take me to the shops," Gwen said once her cousin was gone. She'd overcome her foul mood with shopping, tons of it, filling her bags with clothes, shoes, and jewelry.

One of her favorite designer stores, Versace, had new arrivals, and as usual, she had a personal attendant who knew what she wanted. She emerged two hours later with shopping bags worth thousands of dollars and more to be sent over the following day. She felt much better as she stared at her new bracelet. It glistened with diamond stones. It had set her back ten thousand dollars, but it was worth it, and it made her feel better. Shopping was certainly therapy to her. She had discovered this a long time ago.

Grant and her maids got the bags out of the car and to her closet as she sashayed in, her heels striking against the marble floor. The frown on the butler's face signified trouble, and she had an idea what it was.

"Where is she?" Gwen asked.

"In the study," he replied.

Five years ago, twenty-five-year-old Gwen, daughter of a real estate magnate, met Sir Robert Didier and his wife, Leah, while at a fundraiser. His lineage went back to the Boston Tea Party. Gwen had been attracted to him from the first glance and had noticed his gaze back. Robert had been twenty years her senior, which she didn't care about. She was not surprised when the flowers started coming in or when he asked her out on a date.

A few months later, Leah divorced him. A year later, Gwen was in, married to old money with all the luxury she had yearned for. However, Robert had a fondness for Leah—childhood memories, as he would call it. But this was a thorn in her marriage. She didn't want the ex-wife around her. She knew Leah was up to no good and was plotting her downfall. But Robert thought she was sweet, his best friend who would never hurt anyone. He tolerated all Gwen's excesses and gave her everything she wanted, but the only thing he refused to give into was pushing Leah away from his life. She would trade all her fur coats just to have the woman nothing but a memory. The bitch knew how much her presence annoyed her, and she made sure she was a permanent fixture in their lives—she even had a bedroom in their sprawling mansion.

Leah had been away in Australia on some stupid self-enlightenment journey for the past few months, and Gwen had prayed that she would get eaten by crocodiles. With Leah out of the house, she had been the happiest she could recall, and Robert had listened more to her. She had even gotten rid of the shady décor in the living room, which Robert had kept because his ex-wife loved it. And now she was back! To ruin her life.

Even though she hated the woman, she had to admit Leah did look good for her age. A beauty queen in her younger days, Leah remained slender and stylish in her forties. Her time in Australia had tanned her, but she looked the same as always—annoying. The bitch had the nerve to be seated on her husband's desk, sipping from the old whisky he never shared with anyone. She looked up with a smile, and Gwen could see right through it.

"Gwen, don't you look dashing as always. I see you've done some shopping." She nodded at the Tiffany's bag in Gwen's hand.

"Leah, you're back." Gwen rolled her eyes. She had never bothered to hide her feelings for the other woman, and she knew the woman took great joy in her discomfort. But she couldn't pretend she didn't dislike her.

"Australia was beautiful. The fresh air. The people. You should go there sometime. Now, when will Robert be home? We have a lot of catching up to do. I have a feeling we're going to be talking into the night, so don't expect him to come to bed early." She laughed.

Gwen heard her laughter as she stormed out of the room with clenched fists. One day, she would like to wipe that smug smile off her face. She had thought she was finally free from her. Perhaps Leah would find some hot stud over there and decide to settle in Australia, but she was back and seemed replenished to frustrate her life.

Gwen didn't go down for dinner that night, sulking in her bedroom as she edited the pictures that she posted on social media. Instagram was the best innovation ever. Considered young and hip, she was one of those wives who took advantage of social media; most of her friends didn't know how it worked, and even then, they weren't concerned about using such apps. They'd rather display their luxury amongst themselves. She was, however, one of those few who uploaded everything she did. And Gwen had millions of followers who liked and commented.

She loved the attention she got—the nice comments, even though they were motivated by jealousy, but who cared? She was a celebrity in her own little way, displaying her diamonds, furs, and robes for the world to see. This came with its perks. Despite her husband's money, her followers opened opportunities for her. She got the early release of fashion items, opening tickets without even asking, and, most importantly of all, preferential treatment to the dismay of commoners.

Robert came into the room around midnight. Her nose wrinkled at the flowery perfume Leah wore. That bitch! She must have drowned herself in it. Gwen knew Robert wouldn't be foolish enough to mess around with Leah. He was a highly principled man; he hadn't had anything sexual to do with Gwen until he was divorced from Leah. And besides, he was crazy over her. Yet he was easy to manipulate. She knew this, and so did Leah. Why couldn't he understand the games Leah was playing?

He settled into the bed and stretched his hand over to her. She jerked up and glared. "Go take a bath!"

"But—"

"No! Get rid of those clothes! Burn them, for all I care, just don't come into this bed reeking of her cheap perfume!"

Robert shook his head. "Are we back to that?"

She ignored him as she rested her head back on the pillow. A quiet minute later, he got up and did as instructed. When he returned a few minutes later in his striped pajamas, she could still smell that damn perfume faintly.

CHAPTER 3

GABRIELLE

L aughter rang from the other end of the room, mingling with the rounds of conversation around the dining room. Gabrielle Dodd smiled from where she sat at the end of the table. Her gaze moved from one seat to another. First to the former senator and his wife Shirley before moving on to the other guests. Everyone seemed happy.

Dave leaned forward and whispered, "Good work, honey."

Her smile grew wider. Planning a party, no matter the size, was a chore. Despite this being a success, she doubted she was ready for another any time soon. She was better as a guest than a host. Hosting took weeks of communicating with the caterers, florists, and other staff—ensuring that everything would go according to plan and averting all mistakes that could ruin the night. However, with the calmness and smiles on almost everyone's face, she knew she had done things right.

Gabrielle—well, Gabby, as her close friends called her—followed the clanking of silverware against a wineglass. Charles, an old friend of Dave, wanted everyone's attention. He was charming, and Gabby liked him but not his wife, Amanda, who was stiff. Since the dinner began, she had worn a frown and never concurred as praise was thrown the hostess's way. The woman disliked her and had not hidden it from the first day they had met. Gabby had initially made efforts to be friends, but Amanda had practically slammed the door in her face, not wanting her kind around, which Gabby had heard Amanda say to her husband.

"Dave, you have the best wife ever! Can we do a swap?" Charles teased with a raised glass.

The table erupted in laughter, all but Amanda, whose frown deepened.

"Oh, she's mine forever!" Dave threw back, earning another bout of laughter.

"Thank you for an amazing night, Gabby. We should do more of this," Charles toasted.

There were nods of agreement around the table. Gabby smiled in agreement as well.

The dinner ended at nine, and she stood beside her husband to wave goodbye to their guests.

Her shoulders slumped in relief as she stepped out of her shoes, holding them in her hands as they returned to the house.

Dave chuckled, his arm around her waist. "They're right. You put it all together nicely." He dropped a kiss on her neck.

"Don't be expecting a repeat of it anytime soon. I'll need a three-month interval until the next."

The staff were cleaning the dishes, and she gave final instructions to them before heading upstairs.

"Dave!" she called as she walked into their empty bedroom.

"Out here!"

She found him on the balcony nursing a glass of whiskey.

"The senator and I have a meeting next week. I think he will give his approval for me to join the board," Dave said.

This was great news. Dave came from a political family. His grandfather had been a judge, and his father had been a mayor and had been campaigning for the state senate before he suffered a heart attack. While Dave had no plans of delving into politics, he mingled with politicians who gave him hefty building contracts.

"Mrs. Watson took a liking to you," Dave said.

Mrs. Watson was a retired ballet dancer, and she was a sweet old lady. "Well, I do like her, but I can't say the same for Amanda. I swear her frown could drill a hole in my head."

Dave almost choked as he laughed, spilling the contents from his mouth. He took deep breaths, then said with a grin, "She isn't that bad."

"That's what you think."

Amanda had always disapproved of her. And that was because of Gabby's past. Unlike Dave and his friends, Gabby had come a long way. She hadn't been brought up with nannies or a trust fund. She hadn't gone to a prep school or vacations abroad. She had grown up in a run-down apartment, where clothes hung from windows in a building that reeked of pee and was covered in graffiti. A neighborhood where you needed to be indoors by seven at night, or you could get robbed or even shot. She had watched her mother bring in one boyfriend after another until she had turned sixteen and was kicked out to look after herself. And then she had taken to the streets, trying to survive but always knowing that she would get out of poverty and not end up like her mother.

Due to her excellent grades, Gabby had gotten a scholarship to college. She had gotten the opportunity to mingle with all walks of life, affirming her dream to have a better life. College hadn't been easy, and looking back, she wondered how she had survived.

After graduating from college, she had been faced with the reality that her degree in Fine Arts was a recipe to unemployment and minimum wage. To survive, she had to work two jobs. By day she was an executive assistant, and by night, she was a stripper. She didn't like either job, but she loved being able to pay her rent on time.

Four years later, Gabby had hit the jackpot when a tall man walked into Dazzle Dollhouse, the strip club where she danced. She had danced for him on that pole, her eyes on him all through the night. He came back the next day with his friend Charles. Unlike Charles, who groped the ladies and had been vocal about his needs, Dave had quietly watched her. A week later, he paid for a private session with her. That night, after a quick dance, she went home with him. It wasn't like her to go home with the horny customers, but she noticed something different about Dave. For some strange reason, she felt safe with him. She couldn't explain the feeling; she just knew to trust it.

For over a month, he'd showered her with money and gifts. Even though she'd grown up on the wrong side of the tracks, she had always known how to play the classy game. While her mother screwed a john, she sat in front of the TV watching shows on etiquette. She flipped through society magazines, dreaming of someday being a lady. Her mother laughed when she ate with cutlery or spoke without a Spanish accent. She had always known she was destined for a better life and had prepared for it.

She, however, hadn't expected marriage from Dave. She had suspected he was married, and she was okay being his mistress. When he got her an apartment, she had known she had indeed struck gold. And then along came Amanda.

One afternoon, she opened the door to a pale woman with empty eyes, a woman with a look that said she thought Gabby was nothing but scum.

"I want you to leave my husband, you slut," Amanda spat.

"You should tell that to Dave, not me," Gabby said. She had known this day would come but hadn't been looking forward to it. However, she was ready. The apartment was in her name, and she had been saving her money for some time now.

"Dave?" Amanda said. "I'm talking about Charles. He's been coming here for a week having sex with you."

Gabby had been on a trip with Dave the past week, and although she had been reluctant, she had let Charles use her apartment for his escapades.

So, this was Charles's wife. The boring woman who Charles complained of to the women at Dazzles when he was drunk.

Relief swelled in her. She would have pitied Dave if Amanda was his wife. "Oh, Charles. I don't fuck him. I don't even know who he fucks. He will, however, fuck anything as long as it is female."

Amanda tried to smack her in the face, but Gabby caught the hand before it struck her. The two women glared at each other in rage.

"This is not the last you will see of me! I will make sure you never walk around this city again! You will go back to where you belong, in the gutters," Amanda threatened before slamming the door behind her.

A sobbing Gabby had called Dave, who had hurried over. She had told him the story of Amanda being cruel to her and how she threatened to make her disappear for good.

The following week, she had attended Amanda's birthday as Dave's plus-one. She didn't want to go, but Dave insisted. It didn't help things when Dave introduced Gabby as his fiancée while she was rocking a big diamond on her hand. It still made her burst into laughter when she recalled the pale look on Amanda's face.

Despite Amanda's threats, there was nothing she could do but hate Gabby. Only a few knew of her past. She was a reformed woman who had paid her dues—lessons at charm school and, of course, her natural charm. Not that she cared about anyone knowing her past; it was more or less a grass-to-grace story. But no one would hear of her past from Amanda because it meant Charles's involvement in messing around with strippers would come out as well.

"I'm sure she will come around," Dave said with a shrug.

Gabby didn't care about being accepted by Amanda or her snooty friends. She had a lot of friends, and this was because of her cheery attitude and how she'd always had the ability to make people feel welcome. She didn't like the disdain Amanda treated her with, reminding her of the trash she had come from. When Amanda looked at her, she got reduced to a poor girl in tattered clothes.

"Why don't you go shopping tomorrow? Or go to the spa?" Dave suggested.

Of course, she would love to fill her flowing closets with more shoes and clothes, but it irked her whenever Dave suggested spending money as a way to deal with her problems. When she would get mad at him, he gave her money to go shopping instead of talking things over. She was not complaining, but she sometimes wished he would communicate with her. When someone made her angry, he sent her on vacation. Throwing his money around was his solution for everything, just as he had done when he'd given her a ring after Amanda confronted her.

"That's a great idea," she said with a forced smile.

CHAPTER 4

TRINA

The banging woke Trina Cantrell up. She sat up, eyes wide open in confusion. What the hell was that? The loud noise came again.

"Open up, Trina!"

She grabbed her phone from under her pillow and checked the time. It was almost two in the morning. That bastard! She had waited up for him, called his phone a million times, and had gotten no response. All for him to wake her up when she was having beautiful dreams. She should leave him out there, but she knew he would kick the door down.

She grabbed a robe from a chair and struggled into it as she headed to the door.

"Fucking bastard," she mumbled as she stumbled over a shoe in the dark. She flicked on the living room light and struggled with the numerous locks.

"What took you so long?" Errol glared as he staggered in.

Her nose wrinkled at the foul smell. He was fucking drunk!

"I thought you weren't coming over." She peered around the

street. No one was foolish enough to come to investigate the commotion Errol had caused.

Although he had his apartment—a barely furnished bachelor pad that was usually filled with his homies—Errol spent most of his time at her apartment when he wasn't working or with other women. He said it gave him some sort of normalcy. She had no issue with him living with her as long as he cleaned up after himself and didn't bring any drugs to her home.

"I told you I was coming over," Errol drawled as he pulled her to him, his lips pressing hard on her cleavage.

"You're drunk, Errol," she complained. "How did you even get here?"

"My homeboys brought me over," he said as his kisses rose higher on her neck.

Of course. They had left him dead drunk at her doorstep.

"I want you, babe," he drawled as his lips met hers.

With a frown, she pushed him away. No way was she letting him have sex with her in his drunken state. She grabbed his arm and pulled him to the bedroom. He dropped on the bed with his arms splayed out on both sides. His snores quickly filled the room.

Trina sighed. So many times, she asked herself what she was doing with Errol, aka Eye Drop—his nickname out there in the streets of Detroit. He was sweet when he wasn't drunk, and he was good-looking. He was chocolate brown like she liked her men, and those tats all over his skin made her go crazy. She had been attracted to him from the first day she had met him at a club.

It had been a Friday night, and Trina and her girlfriends had gone to a newly opened club to have some fun. Trina's friend, Sasha, knew the bouncer, so they had gotten into the VIP section. As Sasha walked in, admiring glances and catcalls had been thrown her way. She was a melanin beauty with a D cup and a round ass, more pronounced in her tight, leopard-skin dress.

Errol had been clubbing with his pals, with some skinny woman seated on his lap. All through the night, he had sent drinks to Trina's table; they didn't have to buy one drink for themselves.

After not being able to keep his eyes off Trina, he made his way to their table and wrapped his arms around her waist as her body moved to the fast beat of a rap. She ground on him, her moves growing languid as the tempo slowed.

He had invited her to his home that night, but she turned him down. She had made it clear that she wasn't some chick he met at the club who would screw for the night and forget the next day. Perhaps it was her holding out on the cookie, but he'd been intrigued by her. He had gotten her number from her girlfriend who had gone home with one of his boys, and they had gone out on an actual date a week later, when she was free.

Trina wasn't used to long relationships, usually kicking her partners out a few months later, but she and Errol had been dating for over a year, even though she knew he was screwing other women.

As she stared at him, sleeping in a drunken state, she wondered why she kept him around. Was it because he was a cheerful giver when it came to money? Errol had been selling drugs on the streets since he was fourteen, and now, at thirty-six, he was one of the top drug dealers with many boys under him running the streets. He dealt coke, weed, and ecstasy, but he only partook in the weed. He always said crack was poison.

Errol's lifestyle gave him a lot of cash, which he spent on women, clubbing, jewelry, and drinks. She didn't have to ask before seeing a wad of crisp notes under her pillow. Since she'd started dating him, her life had improved. Her apartment decor had changed, and so had her clothes. But most of all, the change was in her bank account. Her debts were wiped out, and her credit score was improving. When she did kick Errol to the curb, she was still going to have a better life.

But she guessed she wasn't ready to do that yet. She didn't love him— she never had—but he was a great catch in bed. He knew how to manipulate her body, making her scream over and over. She sighed as she sat next to him. She was so tired of men like him, ones she knew she couldn't settle down with In her thirty years, she had dated enough drug dealers, club bouncers, and thugs. There had been a few decent men in between, but she had never been ready to settle down.

Trina was her own woman—an independent black woman who wouldn't take shit from men—most men were all shit anyway, so why stay settled with one? She cooked for her men and cleaned for them, but she called the shots without them even realizing it. A long time ago, she had discovered the power of her body. That with a woman's body, anything was possible. And when these motherfuckers offended her, she knew how best to teach them a lesson. She smiled in the dark. Errol had no idea what was coming his way.

The aroma of pancakes woke Trina the next morning. She sat in bed as Errol moved around in the kitchen, banging away. He was dead wrong if he thought he could calm her with breakfast.

He appeared in the doorway shirtless with a tray. She rolled her eyes. Could he be more obvious?

"Just as you like it," he said, dropping the tray beside her.

He pulled her to him, and their lips met. This time, he didn't reek of alcohol.

"I'm still mad at you." Trina pulled away from him and drove a fork through a sausage.

"I'm sorry. I know you don't like me coming around that late, banging the door, and all that shit. But last night, we had a major deal go through. The homies and I celebrated, and you know how it is." Errol looked at her tenderly with those eyes of his.

Trina sighed. At times like these, he got through to her with that cute look of his. "Fine, but you're still not off the hook," she said with a smile.

Errol laughed, and this time her lips opened to him. Her breakfast forgotten, they wrestled on the bed, her fingers digging into his back as he thrust into her.

An hour later, while he showered, she continued with her breakfast, which had turned cold.

"What are you doing on Sunday? My cousin got a barbecue at his place. You gonna come with me?" Errol asked, drying off his body.

Errol's cousin was a dealer who had hit it big. He had a big house and nice rides. Many in the hood looked up to him. His house was always open for one event or another. She didn't like Riley, but she liked his wife, CoCo, who had one of the best hair salons in town.

"Nah, I got a party," Trina said.

"What party? You never told me of shit like that." Errol frowned.

She paused before she answered. "It's a tea party."

"What's a tea party?"

"It's a party that mostly rich wives host during the day to drink tea and eat scones while discussing their boring lives."

She rolled her eyes as he burst into laughter, his whole body shaking. "A tea party? You fuckin' kidding me!" Errol said, wiping a tear. "What are you? Some black mayor's wife? Even those ladies don't do tea parties."

"Well, I was invited to one. Remember my friend, Gabby, who I met up with a few months back?"

"Ummm... the one who married into money?"

"Yeah. So, she has this tea party thingy she goes to every Sunday, and she invited me."

A brow lifted, and he whistled. "And you gonna go there? You know it's gonna be full of white chicks, cookies, and teas? It's gonna be like those movies where the only black lady serves them tea?" He laughed as he dodged the pillow that went his way.

"Hey! I'm just saying the truth. You gonna choose some boring party over digging it down with real food and black folks? You sure you want that?"

Of course, she didn't want that. She had no idea why she had even agreed to the invitation. It certainly wasn't her scene. She did clubs and cookouts, not some boring-ass party full of wealthy women. But she was curious, she guessed.

Three months ago, she had run into Gabby on the street while she had gone to West Bloomfield Hills on the other side of town from her to visit her rich cousin. She had no idea who was more surprised. She and Gabby had gone to high school together and had been close before Gabby went off to college. The Gabby she had run into was different from the one she had known. She knew the girl was destined for greatness from how she carried herself like a beauty queen. Heck, she'd eaten with fine cutleries at the cafeteria. With her hair pinned into a bun and wearing a fur coat that cost thousands of dollars, she looked ready to be on a magazine cover. Trina had spotted the diamond ring and had summed things up. Gabby had gotten herself a rich man. She had been so happy for her. Out of poverty and into wealth, that was every woman's dream.

She hadn't expected Gabby to hug her and be excited; most women who came out of the ghetto and landed a rich husband looked down on where they came from. Handing her bags to her driver, Gabby had taken her arm, and they had headed to a cafe. Trina never did make it to her cousin's house.

Their meeting had ended with Gabby taking her phone number and promising to keep in touch. She hadn't expected she would keep her word, but Gabby had always been sweet. The following week, they had met and then the next. Although they didn't meet as much as they did when they first reconciled, Gabby kept in touch. Last week she had invited her to a tea party, the Suite Tea Party, to be exact.

"I think you will like it," Gabby had said.

She had no idea why Gabby had invited her. She certainly didn't fit into her world.

"It might not be so bad." Trina shrugged. The truth was, she regretted giving in to the offer. It was going to be a mistake. Was it too late to tell Gabby she couldn't make it?

Errol grinned. "So, you gonna wear a dress? You know those things they wear in those old movies?"

"A frock?"

He laughed. "You even know the shit! You gonna wear the frock thing and a hat? Shit. I gotta be here when you leave. Gonna take a picture and show everyone. Trina the lady."

Errol was still laughing when he left the house to meet his boys. Trina lay on the bed with her hands by her side; she hoped she wouldn't regret this so-called tea party. If those wealthy ladies thought they could treat her like shit, they would have it coming to them. Trina doesn't play.

CHAPTER 5

DANIELLE, GWEN, GABBY & TRINA

Danielle left an hour early; she didn't like arriving late. She was dressed in a yellow floral sundress and black Dior glasses.

Today's tea party was at the Normans' residence. Alicia Norman was the third wife of Thomas, a multimillionaire business mogul in his seventies. His wife was forty years his junior, and although she was loathed by many of the older wives who had been friends with his ex-wives, she had wormed her way into the society.

The Normans lived in a large compound with high fences and a long driveway. There were just a few cars, and Danielle had a feeling she had arrived too early.

There was a tap on her window, and she looked up to a young lad with red hair. It was Alicia's stepson, Logan. He was still in college.

"Mrs. Stanford," Logan said as she stepped out of the car, his eyes raking over her.

"Logan, how are you?" she asked with a smile. She noticed that he wasn't this broad the last time she had seen him.

"Good as always. You look great, Mrs. Stanford," Logan said, leaning forward.

"Thank you, Logan."

"Logan!"

He pulled away with a frown, following Danielle's gaze to his stepmother, who had her hands on her waist. In her early thirties, Alicia was a tall blonde.

"I'll see you around." Logan winked as he got into his red Ferrari.

"I didn't know he was around," Danielle said as she kissed her host on both cheeks.

"You should be careful with that one, Danielle," Alicia said with a frown.

"What do you mean? Is he dangerous? He seems like a charming kid."

Alicia sighed, taking her guest's arm. "You can be quite naïve, Danielle. That so-called kid has had the hots for you since he was a teenager."

Danielle went pale; then, her head turned toward the car off in the distance. "Logan? But he's just a kid! I'm sure he's harmless."

Alicia chuckled. "That's what you think, but I stumbled on his diary and the things I read….I can't repeat them." She shuddered.

She didn't want to argue with her host because it was rude, but she doubted Logan had a crush on her.

A huge foyer opened into the living room with wide windows and doors that led into the garden. However, this was not where they were having their party. She followed Alicia, who talked about the latest renovations, although Danielle barely listened.

Huge, wide doors opened into a hall filled with Victorian chairs and great lighting. The room opened into a wide balcony. Spread on a table were wine glasses, bottles of wine, and trays of snacks. Soft music played from a vinyl record player.

There were three women present. Esther Blake was in her sixties and was the oldest of the members. She was always quiet, either sleeping or crocheting.

Regina Winfield hugged Danielle, smothering her with the heavy perfume she was known for. Regina had been a redhead since she landed her first husband, a failed politician. In her forties, she'd had a streak of wealthy husbands who afforded her a luxurious life and paid vacations overseas. She was chatty, and Danielle liked her; she reminded her of her aunt Macy who didn't give a hoot about what people thought.

"Danielle, I love your sundress. We should go shopping sometime," Regina said.

Danielle smiled politely. She doubted the woman would want to spend time doing so with her. Regina was known for her loud and tight clothes, while Danielle was on the other end of the spectrum.

Danielle didn't know much about Lori Aldrich. She was a quiet woman who only responded when spoken to. Danielle had heard from her mother-in-law that Lori's husband was abusive. While she didn't know if this was true, the woman used a lot of makeup and wore sunglasses all the time.

"We're going to have fun today! I was told we're having someone new!" Alicia clapped with a smile.

Their little circle had grown from three to about fifteen. However, not everyone attended these weekly tea parties. Some stopped by once a month, just as there were regulars like her. She was excited to meet the new person and extend her friendship.

Most of the wives thought their tea parties were a snooty club, and while there were snooty members, it wasn't an exclusive club. But then there were just so many women's clubs out there. She was in a few and had to step away from some—there was usually a lot of competition with literal hair pulling and sides taking. There was a bit of hostility amongst the tea party members, but she guessed they learned to tolerate each other with how few they were.

"How is Brad? Jim said he saw him in Seattle last week," Regina said, referring to her current husband.

Seattle? Brad was in Texas. It had to be a misunderstanding.

"The last we spoke, he was doing just fine," Danielle said. That had been two days ago, and he had been so busy that they could barely talk for a few minutes.

"You must miss having him around. It was the reason I left my third husband. Always about on those awful trips, you know. Leaving me dry at home. He would leave for months and not even a call," Regina said, shaking her head.

Danielle's situation was very much the same as Regina's, but she didn't tell the woman that. She was glad when Alicia produced boxes of bracelets she had bought a few days ago, and the woman's attention moved to them.

GWEN

Gwen left the house late. She usually didn't drive, but she had been furious and had grabbed the key from the chauffeur. It was a surprise she wasn't pulled over with how far over the limit she drove. But then, Robert deserved it if she got pulled over by some stupid cop.

It was all his fault. His ex-wife had ruined her day. It had started over breakfast when Robert had said he was going to a charity function during the week with Leah. Gwen had no interest in going to it anyway, but he should have asked her first. Instead, he had made the decision. She had followed him up to the room, demanding that he change his mind. He had blatantly refused. She had gone downstairs to see a smirking Leah, who must have heard their conversation. All she had wanted to do was smack her in the face. However, she had settled for pouring a cup of wine on her, just in time for Robert to walk in, making her the devil, of course.

He worsened the situation by asking her to apologize. The nerve of him! Of course, she had stood her ground. Until he said he was cutting her off for a week. A week without shopping! A week without going to the spa!

Her hands tightened around the wheel as she pressed on the gas pedal. She was going to make Leah pay. Gwen had been humiliated by being forced to speak those words she never told anyone. "I am sorry." And that bitch had smiled! She had taken pleasure in her disgrace. Oh, she was going to make her pay. She didn't know how, but she would. But whatever she did, she had to make sure Robert would not find out. She was also mad at him for humiliating her and giving her an ultimatum, but it was all Leah's fault. She had to get that woman out of their lives for good.

Leah had returned with more fuel than before, with a mission Gwen could see right through—to destroy their marriage. Leah's plan was not going to work. She had won this round, but Gwen would never again put herself in such a position where she played the fool. She was no fool. She was the queen, and all respected her.

As the Normans' residence gates opened to welcome her, she didn't feel up to meeting with the women. She loved trotting in with the latest fashion design and her jewelry for the week, but she didn't even look her best, wearing a repeat, which she never did. She wanted to be alone, perhaps at the spa, or she could go over to her cousin's. Then she remembered Sophia was out of town. She was here anyway. She would just put on a smile and get it over with.

The door slammed behind her as she got out of the car. She took a deep breath and plastered a smile on her face, but it slipped away. She was more pissed than she realized. She had a terrible temper, and she couldn't hide it most of the time. It had been a long time since she'd let someone get the best of her. That someone who finally broke through should not have been Leah.

"Good afterno—"

"Shut it!" She grabbed the wineglass bubbling with champagne and threw her pink coat on the waiter. "Where are they?"

"Upstairs, first—" the answer came muffled.

She knew where they were. They had held meetings over here a couple of times, and Alicia always had it in the same location.

Some stupid music that made her teeth grit played as she walked in.

"Gwen! You look dashing as always," Alicia said, hurrying over to her.

Gwen liked Alicia. Not because they were married to men older than they were, but because she had a great fashion style. Before Alicia's arrival into Thomas's life, his mansion had been drab and filled with old furniture, but she had waltzed in and changed things. The ladies had met in prep school, although they hadn't been close. They were more of acquaintances still.

"Is that Tiffany's latest?" Alicia asked.

Gwen smiled, lifting her wrist. Her mood was suddenly turning around. "It is. They had it kept for me."

"Oh! I want one. I need to tell Thomas to get me one!" Alicia grinned, her eyes wide in excitement.

Gwen greeted the other women, at least the ones she tolerated, kissed them, then settled down into a comfortable armchair. She was more relaxed now. A sip from her wineglass sent the delicious liquid through her body, warming her up.

Alicia stood in front of them, wearing a broad smile. "I have a lot to fill everyone in on this past week. I don't think I can wait for the others to arrive. I'm pregnant!"

Excited voices filled the room, along with more hugs and kisses. While Norman had three children from his previous marriage, this would be the first for Alicia.

"I know! I know! I'm so excited, and so is Norman. He's so excited that he's going to be a father."

Gwen took a long sip from her glass. Children. She had gone around in circles over having them with Robert for years. He hadn't been able to have children with Leah because of her infertility issues. Thank goodness! If Leah had kids, she would have been an even greater bitch. The thought of that made Gwen shudder.

Children were all cute from a distance. But they were dirty and a lot to deal with, crying all the time with needs. Even if she had a room of nannies, she would still need to tend to a child in the early stages.

No wonder Alicia looked bigger than the last time they had met. She was going to get fat. It was another reason Gwen didn't want to have babies. Nine months was a horrible time to be out of shape. She knew from pictures of her mother that pregnancy wouldn't favor her. She would blow up like a whale and be an embarrassing sight with swollen legs. She knew she could do surgeries to get back in shape. Just another reason for Leah to mock her. She raised her glass in a toast to Alicia's good news. Good luck to Alicia; she had been a fat kid, and she would look even worse than before.

GABBY

Gabby flashed a smile at Trina, who was sitting next to her in her car. "You're going to enjoy meeting the women," Well, she hoped so. She regretted the invitation immediately after it came out of her mouth. She didn't even know why she had invited her. Oh yes, she did remember. The conversation had gotten to a point she had nothing left to say, and it had just spluttered out.

She doubted this was Trina's scene for several reasons. The tea club was not exclusively white. There was Jordan, who was African American, Cheng, who was Asian, and herself, who was Latina, and Meriden, who was Russian, but they were in the minority. She doubted the women cared about race anyway.

Trina looked good in a red gown and black pumps, but it was clear to anyone from a mile away that she didn't fit in. That dress was last season and was bought at a retail shop. The only jewelry she had on was a gold necklace compared to what Gabby had on—her pearl necklace, diamond ring, and emerald earrings. She had pondered it for a minute when she had picked Trina up but then decided against taking Trina shopping for a change of clothes. She knew how proud and confident Trina was and how offended she would be if she in any way suggested her clothes were subpar.

She had mumbled a prayer that the women would go easy on Trina; otherwise, she would have made a fool of herself.

"So, what do you ladies do at these tea parties again?" Trina asked.

"Well, we talk about our week, what projects we are doing, then some talk about our husbands and our families," Gabby said.

"So, kind of like a sorority thing?"

"Not really. In a way, it is, but not really." They didn't have that bond of a sorority, but they had some sort of unity going on for them.

"It will be interesting to see how the other side lives, you know, teacups and all that." Trina laughed. "I can't believe that's your life now, and it fits you well."

Gabby beamed at this. She had always known she wasn't meant for a life of scrubbing dishes or working nine to five. Her mother had called her a dreamer, but she had believed in herself.

"So, are you seeing someone?" There was a lot of catching up to do with Trina. They had been close some time ago, and although she no longer had most of her friends from her old life, she was glad to have Trina around. Trina was cool and could be soft, but she was a no-nonsense kind of person. It was why none of the bigger kids had dared to bully her in high school.

"Kind of, but I'm going to end things with him soon," Trina said.

Gabby chuckled. "You're still the man-eater?"

Trina laughed. "Come on; I ain't no man-eater."

"Right." Trina had broken hearts in high school, not giving a shit about the tears that followed. It always amazed Gabby how Trina could wrap a man around her finger and make him do anything for her, going as far as having one rent a limo for her and her friends for prom. She was fearless.

"Damn! This neighborhood must cost a lot," Trina said as they drove into the gated estate that housed the Normans' house. "You live here?" Trina asked, glued to the window.

"No, but a few minutes' drive away."

Trina whistled. "You know how much these houses cost?"

Gabby shrugged. "I don't."

"What about your house?"

She shrugged again. "I don't. Dave handles all of that."

Trina gave her a look. "So, you don't know how much your house costs, huh? Do you know anything about the bills?"

"Dave handles them."

Trina whistled again. "Must be great not to worry about bills."

Yes, it was. She no longer worried about having her lights turned off or ever paying a bill again. Gabby's husband's office handled all the bills. It was nice.

The Normans' gate opened, and they drove in. She smiled as Trina's eyes widened.

"Damn! This house is fucking grand. Who owns it?"

"Norman, he's into business. He's in his seventies. Alicia, his wife, is our host," Gabby informed.

"She really did strike gold. Waking up every day in this monster must be like heaven."

They were late; Gabby realized as they went around a fountain. Just as she was about to park, a black, shiny Benz pulled in. She sighed; the car belonged to Amanda. Amanda was an on-and-off member of the tea party. She had a feeling Amanda didn't come around much because she couldn't stand Gabby.

"Who's that?" Trina followed her gaze to Amanda, who was getting out of her car in an ugly black dress.

"That's Amanda, my husband's best friend's wife. She doesn't like me. She thinks I'm trash."

"Ahh. She's even glaring toward us."

Indeed, she was. Then she turned around with a huff and hurried into the house.

"Let's go," Gabby said, grabbing her Chanel purse. She couldn't wait to introduce Trina to the ladies.

TRINA

Trina wasn't immune to a life of luxury. She had rich cousins and had dated some rich men, but this was over the top. The estate was loaded with wealthy folks who probably had gold-crusted pancakes for breakfast. She had heard of folks like this but hadn't run into any before. She sure had a lot of stories to tell her friends.

A waiter handed each of them a glass of champagne; the fucking real stuff, not that stuff you got in a box at the local liquor store on the corner. She also took Gabby's coat—Trina wasn't wearing one.

The wide stairs led them to a huge landing, and Gabby led the way while Trina looked around. *Get ahold of yourself,* she scolded herself. None of these ladies needed to know she was from the other side of town.

Conversation ceased as they walked in. All eyes stared at them. Trina had never felt so insecure in her life. She looked good, no doubt, but this room reeked of diamonds and gold. Some of the women looked ridiculous with several rings on their fingers, but they were passing a message—"we are fucking loaded." They looked like Barbie dolls with high cheeks, Botox, and neat hairdos, all with glasses of champagne. It was like she had walked onto the set of Stepford Wives. She looked around; there wasn't even another black person present. Why had she even come here? Barbecue at Errol's cousin's was a whole lot better, even if she had to listen to his dry jokes.

"Gabby!" A woman with a high voice, which made Trina wince, headed for them.

"Alicia," Gabby said, leaning forward to kiss the woman on both cheeks.

Trina was relieved when the woman didn't extend the courtesy to her. Ain't no way she would be kissing some woman's cheeks like she was French.

"Alicia is our host," Gabby introduced.

Her brow went up instantly. This chick had gotten married to a man in his seventies. Okay, her respect just went up a notch. Secure the bag, sis!

"Everyone, this is my friend Trina. I hope you don't mind, but I invited her to join us," Gabby introduced.

"Oh, it is no bother!"

"Your friend is welcome."

Trina resisted rolling her eyes at the cheery voices. These women certainly didn't want her around. It was clear she did not fit in.

"Thank you for having me here," Trina said with a broad smile her mama would be proud of as she dropped into a comfy armchair.

"As I told the other ladies, I'm pregnant!" Alicia announced.

"Oh my! That's so beautiful," Gabby said, hugging the host.

Trina took a long sip from her glass. This woman certainly knew how to play the game.

"Since you are new, Trina, I'll make some introductions," Alicia said.

Passing from one woman to another, Alicia mentioned each woman's name and who she was married to. This all got lost in transmission; the only names she remembered were Gabby, of course, Alicia, and Amanda, who had been scowling at them since they walked in.

"So, tell us about yourself, Trina. What do you do? And who are you married to?" Alicia asked, her eyes resting on her empty ring finger.

"I own my own business. I'm kind of single."

"Kind of single? What's that?"

The woman who had just spoken was pretty with well-arched brows. She looked like she belonged on one of those housewives' reality shows.

"I have a boyfriend, but I'm about to end things with him," Trina said.

"Of course," Amanda said, loud enough.

"Well... that's interesting,' Alicia said, taking control of the conversation. "Aside from the news of my pregnancy, my week has been good. You know I've been working on my charity, and we're going to have an opening fundraiser next week. Isn't that exciting?"

For the next thirty minutes, the women talked about what they had done in the week. It was boring and revolved around the same things— charity balls, shopping, spa, golf, tennis, and horse riding. Trina had spent her week going back and forth with distributors, and it sure wasn't what these women wanted to hear.

How nice it would be to live such a life where you did nothing but useless activities all day, she thought, amused.

"I heard Leah is back in town," a woman with hair in a sleek bun said.

Gwen stiffened at this. "Yes, she is. I thought a crocodile in Australia would eat her, but those things only happen to good people," she said, siping her drink.

"Oh! That's a bad thing to wish on someone," a woman said, her hand on her chest. That was Diana—no, Danielle. It was one of the two. Trina couldn't remember her name.

"Have your husband's ex-wife try to control your marriage, and you'll wish she was dragged to hell by the devil himself!" Gwen snapped.

"Ex-wives can be quite a bore. Like Norman's ex-wife, she keeps asking for more money. She wants this; she wants that. And he keeps giving it to her," Alicia said with a frown.

"At least he gives something. Jerry cut me off," a woman with red, curly hair said.

"Again? This is like, what, the third time in two months?" Amanda said.

"Sandra's husband cuts her off whenever he's angry with work or with his in-laws," Gabby whispered.

Two hours later, the party came to an end with another bout of hugs and kisses. The ladies invited Trina to come back—she doubted they thought she'd take them up on their offer, but she was going to surprise them.

"Did you have fun?" Gabby asked as they drove out of the gate.

"Surprisingly, yes." She had expected to be bored out of her mind, and while initially she had, things had gotten better. Despite their superficiality, they had some good plans for charities. It was a means for them to throw out money, but the charities would benefit anyway.

Listening to their gossip had kept her amused. They gossiped like it was normal, not looking over their shoulders or in a whisper. It came naturally to the conversation.

Trina had learned a lot about people she doubted she would ever get to meet. Who was screwing who. Who was getting a divorce. Who was going bankrupt. And whose child was going to end up in prison for cocaine possession. She also overheard Antoinette Winslow talking to Sharon Waters, and she stated, *"Fred and I went to Sheraton yesterday to see his brother. Imagine how shocked we were to find Jack Field with a young girl. I think she was a call girl."* Trina had a first-row seat to an intriguing movie. It was the white version of a black hair salon where women shared stories of what was happening in the neighborhood.

What captivated her the most was how compliant these women were, Gabby included. They were either rich or had married into wealth. They were mainly beautiful, yet they had no voice in their marriages. Complaining about their husbands cutting them off, about ex-wives having control in some sort of way, and one woman, Nara, even breaking down in tears that her husband didn't have sex with her any longer. These women were the weakest she had ever seen. They had no idea the kind of power they wielded to turn things in their favor.

"Are you coming next week?"

Trina smiled. "I sure am." Errol wouldn't understand, nor would others, why she wanted to be a part of these tea parties. She didn't even know why she wanted to continue coming, but it was what it was.

CHAPTER 6

TRINA

Trina could feel Errol's gaze on her as she put on makeup in front of the mirror. She ignored him, knowing it was just a matter of time before he opened his mouth.

"You sure this ain't a cult or something? Those rich chicks brainwashed you, huh?"

Trina smiled for a second. It seemed that they had hypnotized her, so she would come around every Sunday.

"Cuz, I don't know why you wanna hang out with those ladies? You don't want me around or something?"

Of course, this had to be about him. Men! "Errol, we spend a lot of time together. Almost every fucking night. Now, I'm leaving for a few hours. You're gonna be with your homies anyway." Or one of his women. She had no idea how many there were, but she was sure of one of them. Did it bother her that he had another woman? No, it didn't. She had never had exclusive rights on him in the first place. She usually didn't condone cheating in her partners, but Errol wasn't the kind of man to be faithful. Drug dealers like him felt fulfillment in screwing around with women while they had that one woman they could count on. If only he knew she couldn't be counted on. She was solid and would advise him, but when she was tired of him, she was kicking him to the curb and would get herself a man she knew didn't dip his penis in every woman that walked by.

At her store, she had other options. She had this repeat customer for a few weeks now. He was cute, and she could tell he was doing well for himself. She knew he liked her by those long looks he threw when he thought she wasn't looking. It seemed she had found her next man.

"I don't know why you still go to those boring parties. You said they were stiff," Errol continued to complain.

Yes, they were stiff, but she still enjoyed their company. She had been going to the tea parties for the past three months, and a lot had changed for her.

They had been surprised when she came around the following week, but now, they accepted her with smiles. They didn't look at her with bewilderment or suspicion, although she got the occasional looks at her clothing, more from Gwen. Perhaps they even thought her presence was some sort of charity for them or some kind of diversity. She had a feeling they had resigned themselves to their fate that she was going to be a part of them until she got bored and moved on.

Had she made a few friends? Not really. Gabby was still the person she knew more of, although she liked Danielle, who was way too naïve. It was obvious to anyone who had a brain that those trips her husband was taking were to meet with his mistress. Her least favorite was Gwen. She was a fucking bitch, and every time she opened her mouth, Trina felt like smacking her. But she did like her fashion style, if only she weren't so condescending, looking down on everyone who hadn't risen to her level.

A benefit she had was the information she gathered. These women had no idea how useful they were to her. She doubted they even realized how useful they were in general, perhaps a few of them, but she doubted it. Lori, who was married to a hedge fund manager, had let it slip about some in-house merger of two companies, and Trina had purchased share units prior to the merger at a much lower price. After the merger, shares were five times the price of before. These little bits of innocent information here and there made her decide where to put her money and when to pull out. Rumors of divorce of co-owners of a wine company had made her pull her shares out before that stock tanked.

She took her finances seriously, but not as much as in the past months since she joined the tea party. Now she was taking bigger risks in investments, which meant demanding more money from Errol. He, of course, obliged, giving her the money she wanted.

He kissed her before she stepped out of the apartment with a big bag. She had stopped riding with Gabby, driving her black Sedan instead, which was a sore fit amongst the Ferraris and BMWs.

She smiled at her big bag as she placed it on the passenger seat. A few weeks back, the idea had occurred to her, but now she was confident that the women trusted her. She felt, instead of complaining, that these women needed to take control of their lives. It was time for them to stop playing second fiddles. They had the beauty and bodies to wrap their men around their fingers. But they were just so stiff and naïve. Heck, what she was about to show them would make them run for the hills.

Today's party was being held at Gabby's house, which was beautiful and had a great view of the city. It was so calm and peaceful up there.

Trina was the first to arrive, planning her arrival well. She was just in time to see Dave leave. He exchanged a few polite words with her and left.

"Are you sure you want to do this?" Gabby asked as she added a rose to a collection.

"Yes. I want to do this," Trina said. Some of the women would look at her differently after this, but she didn't care a bit. She didn't even know why she was doing this. Oh yes, she did. It was pathetic seeing these women complain. No one deserved to be miserable when there was a remedy.

She sat comfortably munching a sandwich she had made for herself in Gabby's kitchen. The first to arrive was Danielle. Her husband was away again, and Trina could tell by the frown on her face that she was frustrated.

In a few more minutes, there were more guests, and it was time to set the ball rolling. It started with the usual weekly catching up of how their week went with the same old bullshit.

Then, Gabby stood up and said, "So, Trina has a few things she would like to share with us today. Ummm… I would like us to keep an open mind," Gabby pleaded.

All eyes went to her, with an eye roll from Gwen.

"So, many of you have been complaining about the bad sex you have with your husbands," she began. Voices lifted in murmurs, and she waited for them to die down. She doubted any of them were having good sex anymore, even Gabby, who ought to know better. "Sex is powerful. You should know this. You know how much your husband gives you whatever you want while he's in the throes of passion." She got blank looks and only a smile from Nara. Damn, were these women that oblivious? This was going to be harder than she had thought. "I'm saying you have to use your bodies to manipulate your husbands."

"I don't think I want to use sex to gain favor. That seems like prostitution," Danielle said with nods of approval.

Trina groaned. "Call it prostitution or whatever, but it is allowed in your marriage. It is an old technique used by wives. It is expected of you to do so. Think about when you were younger, and you asked your father for something, and he was adamant that he was not going to change his mind. However, overnight he changed his mind. What do you think caused that? An angel appearing to him?"

Gabby stifled a giggle, but it quickly spread around the room.

"Now that you talk about it, it might be true. One time my father wouldn't let me go on a vacation to Paris, but the next morning he gave his approval," Bernice said.

"How do we do this?" Gwen said with interest.

Probably to get her husband to kick his ex-wife out for good, Trina thought, amused. "First, you must understand that you control sex. I guess most of you are used to your partner initiating sex, right?"

There were nods of approval, just as she had expected.

"When it comes to sex, you need to take the bull by the horns. First, you need to know how to please yourself. Then you will know how to let your husband know how to please you as well."

Trina chuckled at the gasps as she produced a white dildo from her purse.

"What on earth is that?" Danielle asked, her eyes wide open.

"This is a dildo for those who don't know it," Trina educated.

"Bless the Lord!" Lori, who came from an old Catholic family, said, crossing herself.

"I think this is inappropriate. This has never been an objective in this club," Nara said quietly.

"I understand that this must all be new to you, but this is all for your benefit. None of this benefits me. I have a bag full of sex toys I bought with my own money, and I ain't asking for a refund. I have good sex almost every night, so this is all on you. Either you want it or not."

She was met with silence as they absorbed her words. She was just being honest. She didn't like being around such dumb women, but it was their lives to live at the end of the day.

With no objections, she went on "Now, I'm not going to go into the dynamics of how these things work." While she would like to demonstrate so they wouldn't fit the toys into the wrong hole, she was sure one or two would pass out if she pulled her panties down. They would have to figure out the rest by themselves.

"Gabby, why don't you be a darling and distribute those little bags I brought with me?"

Gabby did as instructed. Inside her big bag was smaller pink bags. In each were a dildo, a vibrator, an instruction manual, and a USB thumb drive which was very visual on how to use the toys with added clips of sex scenes. Those who would use them later were going to be wowed with the results.

"This is crazy," Danielle whispered, peering into the bag.

"So, we are supposed to use these, and our lives change immediately? Sounds like bullshit to me," Gwen challenged.

"As I said earlier, first you master your body, and then you will know how to master a man's body. You must learn to give pleasure to yourself before giving to others. You cannot give what you don't have." Her wise words were met with nods of approval. Her days of watching Oprah seemed to be influencing her.

"I want you all to use them this week. You can use it in the bathtub, in your bed, and even in your car if you are confident enough," she added with a grin at the pale looks Lori and Danielle wore. "Next week, we will move to a new lesson."

The conversation continued after she was done, but there was a cloud over them. Her lesson had caused a shift. They were confused and excited at the same time. Some of them wanted to fling their bag into the trash cans, while others couldn't wait to get home. Trina had noticed a few shuffling on their seats. She hoped they would take a leap of faith and receive the blessings that awaited them.

CHAPTER 7

DANIELLE, GWEN, & GABBY

anielle stared at the pink bag for the hundredth time. She had no idea why she hadn't thrown it into the trash when she returned home on Sunday. She wasn't supposed to involve herself with things like this. Brad didn't like it.

She knew about sex toys; her college friends had even kept one or two, but never her.

She looked away from the bag. She needed to decide to get rid of it or not. But why was she so reluctant? Sex had always been good between her and Brad. There were times she never climaxed, but he always did, and that was what mattered. She had been a virgin when she married him, so she had no prior experience. Her mother had given her the wedding-night talk, and it was the same as the sex education she had received in high school.

Danielle had been an avid reader of romance in high school, but she had never felt the nerve-shattering climaxes that the heroines had. And she had accepted her life the way it was until Trina created doubts.

She took a deep breath and reached for the bag. She was going to get it over and done with. Trina had gone to a great deal of work to get these for her, so the least she could do was go through with it.

She locked her room door, even if she knew no one would come in without a knock and a "come in" response.

She poured the items from the bag on the bed, and her eyes widened just as they had on Sunday. Slowly, she reached for the white dildo. It was soft. She had expected it to be hard like wood. It had a rubbery feel, and as she ran her fingers over it, she realized it was an imitation of the real deal. There were two buttons by the balls, and she pressed one. Nothing happened. She pressed the other button. Still, nothing happened. Then she realized it needed two AA batteries.

There was an extra set in the bedside cupboard, and she placed them in the tiny battery space. It fell out of her hand, and she took a step back as the dildo moved back and forth. Her eyes widened. This was so crazy!

She picked up the vibrator next. It was shaped like a rabbit with a cover.

She gulped. She couldn't believe she had such things on her bed. There was a small instruction manual that she read. It was advised to wash the toys in warm, soapy water without the batteries before and after use.

Her hands shaking, she took the toys to the bathroom and ran them through hot and cold water, drying them with a towel and bringing them back to the room.

Trina had said to play the thumb drive on our laptop while using the toys. She stared at the small thumb drive. What was in there? Was it an instruction manual? There was only one way to find out.

She placed the thumb drive in the USB port and returned to the bed just as the screen came on. A woman sat on a bed in black panties and a bra, holding a dildo similar to hers.

The woman smiled, thrusting out her chest. "I'm going to teach you how to get the best orgasms of your life."

Danielle gulped. She felt excited and had a feeling she was going to like this.

GWEN

The only reason Gwen had waited this long to use the sex toys was because Robert had been around for most of the week. Even though the doctor had said she was fine, Leah was under the weather. But she had symptoms, which Robert said his aunt had manifested before she died in her sleep. Every night, it had irked her to wake up to Robert climbing into bed because he had to attend to Leah's whims.

To keep Leah comfortable, there had been changes made in the house. Gwen's beautiful daffodil garden, which she took pride in, had been trimmed because the aroma of the flowers made Leah dizzy.

The menu had to be changed to some horrible meals Leah had picked up in Australia. Gwen's nights at dinner were filled with Leah whining about how miserable she felt with Robert worried and offering to give her a foot rub.

It made Gwen sick. How stupid was her husband? But it made her realize Trina, with her lousy toys and cheap clothes, were right. There was a way a woman could control a man to make him hers. Leah knew the right buttons, and this was how she manipulated her ex-husband; she didn't even need sex to do so. The only woman who needed to control her husband was herself, not some stupid bitch. She was going to get back her man and get the bitch out of her house for good. Leah was getting uncontrollable, and Gwen knew the worst was yet to come.

Robert had taken Leah to the seaside because her lungs needed the fresh air. She was enjoying all this, no doubt. She had made up some stupid excuse to put a bikini on her flabby body, and she had the nerve to wink before getting into the car.

Gwen didn't have to read the manual to know that the sex toys needed to be washed. Who knew where Trina had picked these items up from? Probably some thrift sex toy shop.

She wasn't so stupid that she didn't know about sex toys and porn. Her older brother and father had a cupboard full of porn magazines and movies. However, she had always felt they were beneath her.

Her ex-boyfriends had been good in bed, although she wouldn't give any awards. Robert was traditional in bed; perhaps it was because she never asked, but he'd done things simply and in the same position for as long as they had been married. He didn't even ask for a blow job, and she had never given him one, nor had he put his mouth on her genitals. The truth was she missed all of that, but she had summed it up as one of those things she had to let go of.

Despite putting on a bold front, she had never felt so miserable as she did now. Even the help gave her pitiful looks. She needed to take care of herself and feel good. As well as figure out a way to get her husband out of Leah's leeching hands.

Gwen watched as the woman on the screen, who was some cheap porn star, talked about how to use the toys. She wondered how much she had been paid for this—probably enough to get a day off work.

GABBY

Sex toys and porn were not new to Gabby. Working at a strip club, she knew the dynamics. She had friends who acted in porn, and she had been offered a role several times, but she had always had the belief that appearing in porn would haunt her. Looking back, she seemed to have made a good decision. Stripping for men was more than enough on her resume.

However, despite being a stripper, she had lived a quiet sex life. Perhaps she had her fill with sex with the dancing at the club or the leering of the customers, but by the time she got into bed with a man, she just wasn't up for it. A few men had called her a log of wood of disappointment. A former lover had cussed; he had high expectations, but he'd only encountered a nun. "Except even nuns are horny," he had added.

She had also been a one-girl-one-man woman. A principled stripper, as she had been teased. Her mother's long line of boyfriends had made her stick to that decision. She had only slept with a few patrons, some of whom she had dated later.

However, things had been quite intense with Dave—at least when they first met. They had done it everywhere and in every position, she could think of. He certainly had been a different man in the bedroom, out of control, then the man he was outside, calm and collected.

Now, sex seemed mechanical, and it felt like she was losing his attention. Truth be told, she knew she was in a way responsible. She was no longer the sexy woman he had met; she had let the fancy life tame her sensuality in her attempts to fit in. She lacked that spontaneousness he had admired. What if he got bored of her and found some other woman who was exciting? A woman who knew how to take charge. She knew this wasn't farfetched; there were always women to take her place, hotter than her, who would do anything to be in her position. It was why he had come to the strip club in the first place because he wanted a woman different from those he mingled with.

It was time to get her old self back—well, not the lazy woman she'd been with her other patrons. She needed to keep him engaged with her body. To keep him hot and bothered for her. Like him, she would be a lioness in the bedroom and a saint outside the doors.

CHAPTER 8

TRINA, DANIELLE, GABBY, & GWEN

For the past three months, Trina had been educating the women on how to manipulate their men with their bodies. After the first gifts, the women had returned excited; they wanted more. Only a few of them had not used the toys at the time. Next, she had taught them how to pole dance, and the shocked look on their faces when she emerged in a lingerie coat and stripped to her panties in seconds still amused her.

The women were practicing her lessons in their lives, and it was not only working but also building their confidence. This made them look up to her for advice. However, when she suggested two days ago that the next tea party be held at her house, they looked at each other with surprise.

"Ummm… I don't think that's wise. I mean, where do you even live?" Amanda had asked.

"Probably in a ghetto filled with drugs and guns," Gwen mumbled.

Despite accepting her into their club, they still looked at her as the poor one, which was no surprise because it was true.

Why had she invited them over? Because she hated the long ride to their homes? Or because she hated the luxury glaring in their homes when she walked in? Or was it because she wanted to show them that she wasn't dirt poor like they thought she was? Or perhaps it was just a combination of all.

The idea of a tea party had seemed ridiculous prior, but she had come to realize it was a union for women who were kind at heart, even though they were spoiled and lived sheltered lives. Despite the differences in their lives, the most obvious being the wealth gap, Trina had come to like them. They had shown her their lives, and she wanted to do the same.

There had been a consensus agreement that the meeting would not be held in her tough neighborhood, but this morning, she had gotten a call from Gabby. Call it guilt or whatever, but the women had talked amongst themselves and had decided that some of them would check her house and neighborhood to see if it was comfortable. Their verdict would determine their decision.

So here she was, welcoming Gabby, Danielle, and Gwen into her home. She wasn't surprised Gwen was here. With her high standards, she would tell the ladies that they couldn't be here.

Her apartment looked decent. She had been complimented on the selected pieces she had picked up at the flea market—the armchair, the vintage mirror, and the marble center table. But it paled in comparison to what they had. She wasn't ashamed of who she was or how she lived. And if they dared to look down on her, it was their loss.

However, Trina wondered what they thought of her apartment. It was obvious from the disgust Gwen wore that she hated her apartment; Trina's entire house was probably the size of Gwen's bedroom.

"Would you like tea or booze?" Trina asked as they settled down.

"Anything is fine." Gabby smiled.

"What about you, Danielle? Are you okay?" The woman had been fidgeting since they arrived.

Gwen rolled her eyes. "We had to talk over and over until she decided to come here. She was the only one available," she added.

"Brad will kill me if he finds out I came here," Danielle mumbled, playing nervously with her diamond bracelet.

"He's not even in town!" Gwen snapped.

"He... he got back yesterday," Danielle said, a smile stretching across her face.

Ah! After weeks of being away, he had returned. Of all the ladies, Danielle had the least progress with her husband because he was never around. "Did you have fun with him?"

Her smile was wider now. She nodded. "He was shocked. I did that thing with the tongue you taught us, and he went crazy. I have never seen him act that way before."

The laughter began with Gabby, and soon they were all laughing. Danielle's good news had made them loosen up a bit.

"I think we should have that drink now," Trina said and headed for the kitchen. She had only had a few minutes to get home after leaving work and had been unable to stop by the store to get food to entertain the ladies. However, she had a lot of booze and cupcakes from the lady next door who was blessed with divine baker's hands.

"I must confess, the neighborhood is not as bad as I thought," Gwen said, taking a bite of a cupcake after examining it for minutes.

"What did you expect? The ghetto filled with drugs and guns?" Trina challenged with a lifted brow.

Gwen stared back at her, unfazed. "I guess you live in the better part of the ghetto. The houses are old, and everywhere looks congested, but I guess it would do for someone like you."

Well, if they came at nighttime, they wouldn't be so comfortable. Things could get quite crazy at night, although in the past years, the crime had reduced as the townhouses got taken over by college students and young families.

"So, what has been going on with Leah?" Trina asked.

Gwen sighed. Everyone in the room knew Leah was the only problem Gwen had in her beautiful life. With how selfish she was, Trina was glad about Gwen's problem at times, but she couldn't help but pity her. She'd once had a boyfriend whose baby mama had remained in his life, calling in the middle of the night that she needed things done. It had infuriated her because she had liked him.

Gwen smiled. "I kept Robert indoors for about a week, speechless, of course with orgasm after orgasm. Leah is no longer sick and has been quiet, but I know she's up to something. I can feel it."

"Why not have a baby for him?" Trina suggested. Just as she expected, the woman went pale every time a baby was mentioned.

"No way! So I can be swollen up like Alicia? No, thank you."

"You know if you have a baby for Robert, that will probably get you out of your trouble?"

"How?" Gwen asked with interest.

She sighed. For someone so spoiled, she was stupid. Getting a baby was the first thing Gwen should have done when she noticed Leah's interference. "Leah can manipulate your husband because he has no one to turn his affection to. I know there's you, but he needs more. A child does that. His attention will be solely on the pregnant one. You! You are going to give him the very thing Leah never did. Make him a father. It will make him do anything for you."

The living room went quiet, and she knew the message had been sent clear to all the women. While a child couldn't keep a man, Trina understood their husbands. These men were wealthy and had women willing to be with them. However, they were cut from the same cloth.

They wanted to be in control. They wanted someone to look up to them. A child was that someone.

"I will think about it," Gwen said with a shrug.

It was her loss. Either she fought back smartly, or the other woman would stay in her home.

"Is there more where this came from?" Gabby asked, nodding to the empty tray of cupcakes.

It was just her luck; there were more in the kitchen.

"Don't worry, I'll go get it myself," Gabby said, taking the tray with her.

"So, I've been thinking about Alicia's shower, and—" Danielle began but paused at a sound in the kitchen, like the back door that led to the small backyard was being opened. "—I think we should hold it at our country home. You have never been there, Trina, but it is gorgeous. You will love it. Oh my God!" The glass slid from Danielle's hand to the ground, the liquid spilling over her.

Trina gasped. Gabby had returned to the living room, but she wasn't alone. With her were five men, all masked. There was a gun to her head.

"Oh, God! We're going to die!" Danielle sobbed.

Gwen shot Trina a dirty look that said, "I knew this would happen."

Trina took a deep breath. In her five years living here, there had never been a break-in. Never! The last time she had been robbed was when she was a teenager.

She eyed the men, and she knew the ladies were outnumbered.

"Ha! What the hell is this shit? What you bitches doing here?" the one holding a gun to Gabby said in a gruff voice.

"We are having a tea party," Trina said slowly.

The leader laughed, and the other men joined in. "Fucking tea party! I don't even know what that is. You ain't supposed to be here, lady," he said with a nod at Trina.

Oops. It was terrible timing. She had put things together and realized this wasn't about her. This was about Errol. He had brought trouble to her doorstep.

Another man joined them and jolted in his steps. "Who the fuck are these white bitches?"

A short man said, "Eye Drop's lady got loaded, white friends. Check out these diamonds."

Danielle screamed as the diamond-studded necklace got ripped from her neck.

"Any of you fucking scream, and I will blow your fucking heads off. Understand?"

The women nodded in understanding. These men meant business.

"Dre, grab a bag and get every piece of shit they have on them. We just hit the jackpot!"

The men hooted in agreement

Danielle continued to sob as she was emptied of every piece of jewelry she had.

"Don't touch me with those filthy hands!" Gwen pushed a hand away. "I will give them to you." With her head raised high, she took her time removing her jewelry and throwing them with a clank into the black bag.

With the women emptied of their jewelry, all eyes rested on Trina. She had some cheap gold necklace on, and she removed it and handed it to the short man.

"The ring?" the leader said.

God! She had been hoping they didn't spot it. It was a diamond ring, and it had belonged to her mother; her father had saved up for it when times were good.

She pushed back tears as she slid it from her fingers and handed it to the short man.

"Thanks for making us rich, bitches. Come around next time, huh?" the leader said with a chuckle that travelled around.

As he turned around, Trina spotted the tattoo peeking from his arm. She knew who he was. Blu had grown up with Errol, and they had run the streets together. But they'd had issues and had become enemies.

"Oh, God!" Danielle slumped to the ground as the kitchen door closed.

"You set us up! You did this, you conniving bitch!" Gwen glared.

"Brad is going to kill me! They took my wedding ring!" Danielle cried.

"Stop crying like a baby! They fucking took my Tiffany necklace I bought yesterday! You are so screwed, Trina! You are so fucking screwed! I'm going to call the police, and you and your gang will end up behind bars," Gwen threatened.

"Are you sure you want to call the police?" Gabby asked, taking a big gulp from the bottle of whiskey.

"They will get our things back!"

Gabby chuckled. "There will be consequences for this. First, our husbands will go crazy if they find out we came here. Second, the police won't pay us any attention, and we will only invite unnecessary attention to ourselves."

"Then what are we supposed to do? I can't go home like this! That was Robert's grandmother's ring! With all this going on."

"That was my mother's ring," Trina said quietly.

"That was a marble stone, and you should give—" Gwen added.

"Will you shut up for a second! Shut the fuck up! I've had it with that screeching voice of yours! You think I would set this shit up? Because I fucking didn't. I'm not stupid or greedy enough to bring you to my home for that shit!"

Even Danielle went quiet at Trina's yelling. Gwen took a deep breath and relaxed on the couch with a faraway look.

"Do you know who they are?" Gabby asked.

Trina nodded. "My boyfriend, Errol, he deals drugs."

"Of course," Gwen mumbled.

"That was his enemy, Blu, and his gang. This has never happened before. Never. I guess they thought the house would be empty and planned to break in. They had no idea we would be here."

"Is there any way we can get our things back?" Gabby asked.

Trina sighed. "I don't know, but I'm going to talk to Errol. He should be able to get them back for us. I'm sorry, ladies. Never would I ever do such a thing to you."

Gabby nodded. "We must go, Trina. Talk to Errol. For now, we might be able to give excuses for our missing jewelry, but it won't hold for long. If we don't get them back, we're doomed."

Trina didn't see them off to the door. She was too weak to do so. After the door closed, she flung an empty flower vase against the wall.

She was embarrassed about what had happened. She couldn't believe those bastards had dared to bring the battle to her. Those poor women didn't deserve to be exposed to such danger. It was fitting for them to suspect her, but she wasn't that greedy, and she didn't do things that way.

She reached for her phone and called Errol. His phone rang twice before her call was picked up.

"Who this?" asked some gum-chewing woman.

"Put Errol on!"

"Who the fuck are you to Errol? One of his side pieces, huh?"

She hung up. She was even more pissed. So, he was screwing some heifer while she got robbed? She should have gotten rid of him a while ago. She took a deep breath. This needed to be fixed as soon as possible. She knew Blu and his crew would sell the jewelry soon enough, and then it would be difficult to get the pieces back.

She was going to wait for Errol and make him get their stuff back. She grabbed the bottle of whiskey and took a long sip from the bottle.

CHAPTER 9

DANIELLE, GWEN, GABBY, TRINA

"A re you okay?" Brad asked.

Danielle looked up from her breakfast and flashed a quick smile. Inside, her nerves were a mess. Yesterday she had paid a visit to hell. It was a surprise she hadn't fainted right there. She had been robbed of all the jewelry she wore! This meant she was unable to function properly. Last night, she remained stiff in bed, and Brad looked disappointed.

Perhaps she should tell him. But she quickly stopped herself. On the ride back home, she and the others had agreed that they would tell their husbands that their jewelry was being cleaned. That would give Trina's boyfriend some time to get them back. If Brad found out where she had been, he would be very pissed, and she knew that would push him away even more.

Her phone buzzed, and she reached for it. She had been added to a private group with her, Trina, Gwen, and Gabby as members.

Gwen: *Have you gotten our jewelry back yet?*

Gwen had been livid on the ride back. She hoped she wasn't naïve with her trust and that Trina was innocent. She believed Trina had set the robbery up, but Danielle doubted it, and so did Gabby, who claimed to trust her.

Trina: *He didn't come home last night. He did call, but I couldn't tell him over the phone. Something is going down with them. A crackdown by cops or something like that. So, he needs to stay on the low.*

Gwen: *How convenient. I will make sure you never walk into any restaurant in this city again.*

The ladies had agreed not to tell the other club members what had happened. If they did, their husbands would be aware by nightfall.

Trina: *There's a way we can get them back.*

Gabby: *How?*

Trina: *By ourselves*

Gwen: *So, you are also crazy?*

Trina: *As I was saying, no one will help us but ourselves.*

Danielle: *So, you're saying that we four women should go up against five or more armed men?*

Gabby: *I stand with Danielle and Gwen; this is crazy, Trina. These are very dangerous men.*

Trina: *If you want to get your jewelry back, meet me at noon. I will send you the address.*

Danielle sighed. She didn't like where any of this was headed, but she had no option but to meet up with Trina. She felt so naked without her diamond-studded necklace and wedding ring. It was the only way she could get her jewelry back.

"Your finger looks bare without your wedding ring," Brad said.

After what had happened, she just didn't feel like wearing any jewelry.

"When did you say you were getting it back again?"

"In a few days," she said into a teacup.

Hours later, Danielle slid her car into a vacant spot at a shooting range. She toyed with the strap of her purse as she got out. Was Trina serious about this? Her phone rang. It was Trina asking where she was; the others were with her inside the range.

Gabby had no jewelry on, but Gwen, of course, had a pair of golden earrings, a pearl necklace, and a bracelet with an emerald.

"First of all, this is a ridiculous idea," Gwen said.

"I know it is, but there's a huge chance of success with this. I have a feeling it is going to work," Trina said.

"And if it doesn't work?" Gabby asked.

Trina sighed. "Let's be hopeful, okay? Who knows how to shoot?"

Gwen raised her hand. "What? Don't be surprised. My dad used to hunt boars with his clients, and I tagged along."

"How good is your aim?"

Gwen grinned, sending chills down Danielle's spine. "I hit a boar right between its eyes."

Trina nodded. "I haven't used my gun in a while, but I usually come here. Danielle and Gabby, you girls are going to learn how to shoot. Nothing serious, but to give you enough knowledge about what to do. We might not even have to use the guns, but we need to be prepared. Let's go," Trina said.

The women had shot downrange repeatedly until they got the hang of it. And it had certainly not been easy. Despite the earplugs, Danielle's ears still rang. She hoped if the need arose, she wouldn't freeze, unable to pull the trigger.

Trina hired Angel, a former police officer. She was going to teach them self-defense. Angel exchanged small conversations with Trina, who was on intimate terms with her, and they talked about mutual friends before they got down to business.

By the time they emerged from the studio, it was getting dark; Danielle was tired, sore, and brimming with the knowledge she hoped she would remember.

Despite their murmurs of being tired, Trina talked them into going to a small cafe, which was empty except for them.

"So, what is the plan? You never told us," Gabby said, biting into a burger that looked yummy, but Danielle had gone with a salad.

"Tomorrow we are going to strike. Tomorrow at noon," Trina said.

"We should do it at night," said Gwen, who had ordered a bottle of water.

Trina shook her head. "No, it would be suicide at night. Too many men around and their bitches. We won't be able to take them on then. This is how it is going to work," Trina said, leaning closer.

G W E N

Gwen had woken up in the middle of the night to a scream that had Robert running to Leah's room. He returned an hour later; Leah had a horrible nightmare. No words, Gwen returned to sleep. She had no care for Leah until she got her jewelry back.

"As I was saying, I'm looking forward to lunch with the Harrys. They have always been old friends of ours," Leah repeated for the hundredth time.

Gwen knew she was trying to rile her up to whine that she hadn't been invited by the Harrys who didn't like her, but she just didn't care. The woman threw her a look, probably trying to figure out what was wrong with her.

As ridiculous as Trina's plan was, it might just work. She couldn't recall the last time she had been this excited, especially at the shooting range. Robert never took her shooting with his friends; it wasn't a woman's place.

What they were going to do was so crazy! And if it worked? Well, that would be even crazier. She didn't want to think of what could happen if it didn't work. Well, this would be the last time she listened to yapping Leah. However, she would haunt Leah from the beyond; there would be no peace for her and Robert.

"I'll see you, hon," Gwen said, dropping a kiss on her husband's head.

"Where are you going?" Leah asked.

Gwen smiled. "Shopping, of course." And with a twirl, she was gone.

The chauffeur had the day off, so she drove to the country club to meet up with Danielle and Gabby. In the restroom, they changed into the black T-shirts and pants Trina had given them last night. With their cars left with the valet, they got into a cab and headed to Trina's house again.

"This better not be a repeat of the other day, or I will kill Trina myself," Gwen stated. And somehow, Danielle and Gabby believed she would.

Trina was in her bathrobe when she let them in, sipping a cup of tea.

"You all look great." She smiled.

"Where did you get this T-shirt from? It's itchy," Gwen said.

Trina only smiled, and Gwen couldn't help but smile. She was supposed to be mad at Trina; after all, it was her who had gotten them in this mess, but yesterday's events had Gwen pumped up.

It took Trina an hour to get ready, and she joined them in the living room in a similar black T-shirt and pants. She had with her a big black bag. She poured the contents on the couch, and Danielle jumped.

"Where did you get those from?" she squeaked.

"Last night, I got these for us. We can't go in without them,"

Trina said, handing each woman a handgun. "They're loaded, but we'll take extra bullets with us." Next, she gave the ladies Tasers and face masks to conceal their identities.

"Last," she said, handing out earphones. "We need to stay connected all through. Now let's go over the plan again before we leave."

When they arrived, Gwen noticed a black truck with tinted windows parked in front of Trina's house. Trina unlocked the doors, and the ladies jumped in. "What happened to your vehicle?" she asked.

"I swapped it for today. My car might be easily spotted," Trina said, getting in.

Gwen sat with her in the front, and the others were in the back with the windows rolled up.

The streets got busier as they left Trina's neighborhood. Gwen stared; this was the real ghetto. The houses were clustered with clothes hanging from windows. Graffiti covered buildings with windows missing or boarded up. Music played from different directions. Children played while young men rallied in groups rolling dice on the ground.

The car came to a stop, and the ladies looked at Trina.

"You see that brown building?" Trina asked, pointing ahead.

They all nodded. In front of the building was a group of guys rapping.

"That's Blu's crib. We're going to go around and get in through the back," Trina said.

Even though the windows were tinted, Gwen gulped as they drove past the house. There were so many guys who she presumed were street gangsters out there; would they be able to take them all?

Trina went down the street and parked in a position that gave them a good view of the building. Then Trina made the call.

They waited thirty minutes before a bike approached. On the back seat was a pile of pizza boxes. A woman wearing a helmet got off it, and she talked with the men for a while. Gwen wondered what they were talking about.

"You think they're going to believe one of them ordered pizza?" Gabby asked.

"You think thugs don't eat pizza? There are so many of them; they won't know who ordered what. All they care about is getting through the boxes," Trina said.

"Won't she get in trouble?" Danielle asked.

Trina chuckled. "Raven is trouble. Besides, she leaves for basic training in the military tomorrow. No way they're gonna get her."

"How again do you know her? And why would she do this for you?" Gwen asked.

"For us," Trina corrected. "We go way back, and she owes me a favor."

There was a story there, but she doubted the woman would say more. Her shoulders relaxed as Raven got back on the bike and zoomed off. The men passed the pizza boxes with a few taken inside. Out of nowhere, cans of beer emerged. It was such a party that Gwen smiled.

Trina's phone beeped, and she glanced at it. "It is Raven. She said we're good. They were excited about the pizza, no questions asked."

"How long will it take for the drug to take effect?" Gabby asked.

"Thirty minutes tops. Remember, we get in and get out as soon as we can. No delays. We know what we're looking for."

One of Blu's girls had rattled out about the layout of the house, where Blu stayed, and where he kept his stolen property. He loved having them around him, which meant they wouldn't have to break through a safe.

The wait in the car was quiet. Gwen was calm on the outside, but she was nervous. She wanted this done with. She hoped nothing bad happened to her or any of them. They were waltzing into the lion's den.

"It's time," Trina said.

Gwen jolted from her thoughts. She hadn't realized the time had gone by that fast. There was no one at the front of the building—well, except for the two slumped in front of the stairs.

"Let's go. We got about thirty minutes before someone notices something is wrong and heads over. Remember, not everyone might have eaten the pizza, so we need to be very careful," Trina said, igniting the engine. They drove to the back of the buildings. There was a high mesh fence that wasn't locked.

"I think we should pray before doing this," Danielle whispered.

"Good luck, everyone," Trina said, pulling her mask down over her face

The gate swung open at Trina's push, and quietly she led them into the devil's den. The kitchen door opened at Trina's kick, and they followed her in.

In the kitchen, two women in shorts and camisoles sat sleeping in their chairs in deep slumber. The kitchen led into a dark hallway that opened into a wide sitting room. It was like an orgy, only with sleeping bodies. It seemed the pizza had gone round.

There was a noise, and the women froze. It was coming from upstairs. A shadow emerged from the stairs.

"Who the fuck is—"

Danielle leaped and tasered him, and the man dropped. Gwen's brow lifted. *Go girl*, she said silently.

While Danielle and Gabby tied him up, she headed upstairs with Trina, their steps quiet.

Loud music embraced them, and she shared a look with Trina. They needed to be careful. There were a lot of doors on this floor.

The one closest was open, and she peeped in. On a bed with a naked, sleeping man were two girls, sleeping as well. On a table was white powder, which she knew was cocaine. This was so fucking crazy! A week ago, Gwen had lived a rather innocent life, and now she was in a feared drug dealer's house with a gun.

Her heart raced as they approached the door at the end of the hall. Anyone could leap at them from one of the rooms, but their descent was quiet.

Trina pointed at the door and did some silly sign with her fingers. What did that even mean? Before she could comprehend what she meant, Trina kicked the door down.

Two girls in bra and panties stared in shock at them. Their hands were filled with money they were stuffing into a bag from under the bed. Lying on the bed was a man sleeping with deep snores.

Trina nodded at her. This was the mighty Blu.

"I see you decided to have some fun for yourself, ladies—Smart of you. Now move to the side before I blast a hole through your skinny heads," Trina snapped, pointing her gun at them.

"Please… please don't kill us," the one with green hair pleaded as she went on her knees.

Gwen growled. The bitch had on her diamond necklace! She was going to kill her!

The girl squealed as Gwen grabbed the necklace from her neck, not caring about the latch.

"Where is the other jewelry?" Trina asked.

The other girl pointed at a wooden chest that sat on a drawer. With her gun and gaze on the ladies and the door, Gwen went to it. Her heart leaped with excitement when she opened it. Her ring was in there! She had missed it so much!

"Is everything in there?" Trina asked.

She quickly ran through the contents. Underneath their stolen jewels was a bunch of jewelry probably stolen from others.

"Yes, with other stolen items," she informed.

"A car just pulled up at the front," Gabby's voice came over the earphone.

"There's no time to separate them, just grab the box!"

Trina clutched it to her chest.

"Now remember, ladies, we weren't here. Understand?" Trina asked.

They nodded in unison.

Their feet hit hard against the wooden floor as they raced downstairs.

"You got it?" Gabby asked her eyes on the door.

"Yes. Let's go before they come in," Trina said, running down the hallway and out the kitchen.

Immediately they got into the truck, the tires screeched, and they were off. No one said a word as Trina drove like she had ants in her pants.

It was only when they pulled up in the parking lot of a McDonald's that they let it out.

"Oh my God! We did it!" Danielle danced in her seat.

"Yes, we did! We fucking did it!" Gabby ripped the mask off her face.

"And we didn't have to kill anybody. Do you think the man I tased is okay?"

Everyone went silent; then they burst into laughter.

"Thank you, Trina," Gwen said. She had no idea who was more shocked of them all. But really, she was grateful to Trina.

"So, I can walk into any restaurant I want in peace?" Trina asked with a smile.

"I'll think about it," Gwen smiled.

"Let's get our jewelry out of the chest and ditch it," Danielle suggested eagerly.

All their jewelry was in it, and in a few minutes, their rings were back on their fingers, earrings on their earlobes, and necklaces on their necks.

"I can't find my mother's ring," Trina frowned, digging into the chest. She huffed for a few more minutes and sighed. "It's not here."

"I'm sorry about that, Trina," Danielle said.

"Yeah," Trina said after a moment. "We win some; we lose some."

"So, what do we do with the rest of the jewelry? The ones that aren't ours?" Gwen said, eyeing a gold bracelet. It looked cheap, but it would look good around her wrist.

Trina slammed the box closed and handed it to Danielle, who took it with a puzzled look.

"A time will come when we might need it. Let's take it as our bargaining chip," Trina said as she started the car.

"Where are we going?" Gabby asked.

"To celebrate, of course." Trina smiled.

ACT 2

DANIELLE'S
BLACKMAILER

CHAPTER 10

TRINA

The voices buzzed around Trina as she sipped from her glass of wine. They were debating how to celebrate Alicia's baby shower. Some of the women wanted a casino theme, while others wanted a Cinderella shower. She didn't care about what they wanted. As much as she wanted to be around the yappy women, Trina was going to be busy the night of the shower, although she hadn't expressed her future absence.

Her eyes met Gabby, who flashed her a smile. It was three weeks since the incident—the incident of them going into Blu's territory and getting back their jewelry—and they hadn't talked about it since. It was an unspoken secret, but she knew soon they would have to address stealing their jewelry back. She could feel the tension whenever they spoke, a spark waiting to be ignited.

The ladies had decided not to mention anything to the other ladies at the Suite Tea Society either. It was not as if Blu, the gangster that robbed them at Trina's house, would hear about their involvement, but sharing such a delicate matter with others was stupid. The ladies had agreed to tell the club members that Trina's house was comfortable but too small to fit all of them. Most of them had given her looks of pity; she was sure they would have brought out their checkbooks to contribute to the rent for her to move to a bigger and better place if not for the scowl she wore.

As much as Trina wanted to have them over at her home, it wasn't safe. Blu had no idea that Trina and her friends were responsible for the attack. Word on the street was that some mercenaries from out of town had hit them, but no one knew who had hired them. Still, she couldn't risk putting the women in danger. If something did happen, she had no idea if she would be able to control it. So, into the trash can went her idea of entertaining them.

"What do you want, Trina?" Alicia asked. "A casino or a Cinderella theme for my shower?"

Trina shrugged. They were grown-ass women, so what were they doing with a Cinderella theme? "A casino any day."

Celine, who was rumored to be a gambler and had been in and out of rehab, whistled, giving her a thumbs-up.

"A casino wins then!" Alicia clapped as Trina realized hers had been the winning vote. "I know just the place to throw the party. A real casino! We will go to one of the best casinos in Michigan and win all the games!"

Shouts of glee followed her announcement, and Trina smiled. It seemed like fun, although she was sure most of the women would lose more than they would win. None of them looked like they knew much about gambling. But then, they could surprise her.

Trina said her goodbyes with hugs—she still wasn't used to the kisses. Her relationship with the women, especially Gwen, Danielle, and Gabby, had become intense in the past weeks. Since the incident, she had forged a strong bond with the trio; it wasn't obvious, but they had formed a clique of their own, hanging out during the week and sharing lame jokes in their group chat. She was becoming quite fond of them. Her black friends couldn't believe she had rich white friends. But theirs was a relationship she couldn't explain.

Errol was at the front door when she returned home. She rolled her eyes as she stepped out of the car. She had broken up with him three days after recovering their jewelry. Their breakup was long overdue. She knew he hadn't seen it coming, and he had pleaded to get back with her, but she just wasn't interested. Being with him was a reminder of the danger of dating a drug dealer. If Blu could break into her home, others would not mind using her as a pawn when needed. This was the first time she had ever been caught in the middle of a fight with a drug dealer and his enemies, and she had a feeling if she stuck around for much longer, things would get messier. When Errol had dropped by the night of the incident, Blu had given him a call, warning him that he would retaliate. Errol looked lost, as he had no idea what had happened, and Trina sure wasn't going to be around when shit hit the fan.

"Yo, Errol! What do you need?" Trina asked, sliding her key into the door. She had not only taken her keys from him but had also changed the locks—not that it would stop anyone who wanted to break in. Her security system will be up and running for added measures next week. It wasn't until recently that she could sleep well at night. After the robbery, she had developed a habit of waking up at the faintest sound, and she kind of missed having Errol next to her in bed.

"I forgot my hoodie, you know, the red one."

She sighed. She had converted it to hers. It was a comfortable hoodie that had a black panther on the front. But if he wanted it, she should give him his shit so he would head out.

"You not gonna ask how I've been doing?" Errol asked as she walked to her room.

With her hands on her waist, she turned around. "How are you, Errol?"

"Tired. Shit hasn't been easy. The streets are tough. You know that shit that went down with Blu?"

She nodded. How could she not know?

"We fucking on guard now 24/7. I haven't gotten sleep in days. Word is that the feds are in town. You know, no one is talking, so the homies are on edge. You know, someone did a big one on Blu. Drugged the shit out of him and his homeboys and stole all the money they had with them. The bastard thinks I did that shit, and he's gonna hit us. Fucking idiot!"

Whenever Errol talked this much, it meant he was heavily stressed. She noticed the lines and bags under his eyes. He hadn't even shaved in days. She would have pitied him, but she was amused. The gangsters were on edge because of them. Laughter bubbled in her throat. Over four women! Women they would ignore on a normal day.

The hit on Blu was all the neighborhoods could talk about, even weeks after. No one knew what had happened, and she didn't blame them. Blu had been reluctant in admitting that he and his crew had been drugged via pizza. Some folks were calling him and his crew "sleepy head" on the street, although not to his face. He was pissed about the hit and had placed a bounty for information. But no one knew shit, apart from her and the trio. Trina had made sure of that. The smaller the circle, the better kept a secret. She was pretty sure Blu had made calls to the pizza place, but there was no trace back to Raven, who was now at the Fort Bragg, North Carolina military base. Besides, no one in Blu's crew had ever seen her face. Everything would lead to a dead end.

While Trina would like to correct Errol and everyone that she and her friends had only taken the jewelry, pride swelled for what those drug ladies in the house who had been awake had done; they had probably stripped the place of all cash before the others woke up.

Thumbs-up, girls! They were not stupid, and that was the way to survive out there.

Errol waited in the living room as she headed to her room to get the hoodie, but when she reached for it in her closet, he snuck up behind her and wrapped his arms around her waist. She had been expecting this.

With a glare, she pushed him away. "Take your hoodie and leave, Errol!"

"Come on! Why are you acting so cold toward me, huh? You know you want me, and I want you too." Errol grinned.

"Why don't you go meet one of your hoes to screw around with?"

Errol groaned. "Come on! This still about that bitch? I told you she's nobody. You're not the type to be jealous anyway."

She closed her eyes and took a deep breath. "Look, Errol, we're done. We had a good time together, but we always knew it would end. Let's move on from this. You'll find some hot lady to fuck, and I'll find someone to love me. Okay?"

"Fine," he mumbled, accepting that they were through. "You need anything, holla, you hear? Money. Protection. Even good dick. Imma be there for you. Don't be a stranger. And keep the hoodie. I know you love that shit."

He gave her one last hug, and she swatted his hand away as he tapped her ass. It was great to see him out the door. It had been fun while it lasted.

She did some chores she had left all week, then planned for the following week. Owning a boutique had always been something she wanted; she sucked at designing clothes but did have a good eye for quality clothes. Most of her wares were made by black designers in her aim to support black businesses. A new shipment was coming in that week, and her customers were excited to see it.

Her phone buzzed. It was a message from Hannah, one of the

women at the tea party. She had gone shopping for lingerie and had sent some choices for Trina to see if she liked them or not.

Hannah: Which one do you think John would like?

The women looked to Trina for advice, especially as their husbands reacted to them more. This meant more shopping allowances, trips, and freedom for some of them. But Trina wanted them to take more control. Be bosses—own businesses aside from charities. Most of them were on the board of directors and owned shares, but they had no say in their companies, mainly because they had relegated their powers to their husbands, brothers, or fathers. She didn't want them to feed on grains left on the ground but eat directly from the table. It wasn't going to be easy, especially with their indoctrination from birth, but she could feel their resolution breaking.

CHAPTER 11

GWEN

"I'm pregnant," Gwen said, right before pushing a spoon of oats into her mouth.

Food particles flew out of Leah's mouth, and Gwen moved away before it could splatter on her. The woman went pale, and Gwen smiled. Oh yes! Victory sure felt good.

"You're pregnant?" Robert asked in a whisper, his eyes wide.

"Yes, I'm—"

She squealed as he lifted her from the chair, twirling her. She had never seen him this happy, his face lighting up with glee.

"We're pregnant! We're pregnant!" Robert sang.

If she had known he would be this happy, she would have gotten pregnant years ago. She had stopped taking birth control and worked toward getting pregnant from the day Trina brought the idea up. Three days ago, she had started feeling queasy and had made an appointment with her doctor. Voila! She was pregnant. It still seemed unbelievable that she had a little brat growing inside her.

"We're having a baby! Leah, we're having a baby!" Robert said, hugging his ex-wife.

"Yes, you are," Leah said with a smile, but Gwen could see through the smile. The woman was pretty shaken up.

"This is amazing! I'm going to be a father!"

"I thought you didn't want to be a mother. You said children were beneath you," Leah said before taking a long sip from her glass.

Gwen smiled broadly. "People change, don't they? I have decided I want to be a mother. That I want to fill this house with little brats. Little Roberts and Robertas."

Robert chuckled. "I like that. Roberts and Robertas." He took her hand and placed a kiss on it. "You have given me great news today. The best ever!"

She wasn't the crying type, but tears welled in her eyes. If she had known he was this passionate about having children, she would have given him one or two and had her tubes chopped off. "Why didn't you tell me you wanted children?" she asked softly.

Robert shrugged. "Leah and I couldn't have children, and I guessed I accepted my fate when you were against having them."

"Oh, I'm going to give you your heart's desire," Gwen said, directing a look at Leah.

Leah had been a bitch for the past three weeks, finding ways to rile Gwen up. And she had endured while she patiently planned on the perfect way to kick Leah out of their lives for good.

"I'm going to get the cabernet sauvignon. This calls for a celebration. You're not drinking, of course." Robert frowned at her, then danced off with a smile.

"You're making a mistake. You will make a horrible mother. You are selfish and spoiled!" Leah spat

Her words hit Gwen. Despite the harshness, there was some truth in what Leah said. Would she make a good mother? Or raise horrible children who would turn out to be psychopaths?

Leah cackled, clearly seeing doubt on her face. "You have enough time to get rid of it and keep your figure. Don't make a lifelong mistake. Children are not things you can return to a store when you have had your fill."

Gwen sneered. As much as Leah's words were true, she could see right through her. "I will deal with the consequences, Leah. Sadly, you were never able to give Robert children. Why not keep your thoughts to yourself? You cannot give what you never had," Gwen said, softly rubbing her stomach. Leah's eyes flashed in rage, and Gwen smiled.

"Here it is! A wine to celebrate. When my son is born, I will tell him his father opened a befitting wine in his honor," Robert said, placing the expensive bottle of wine on the table.

"What if it's a girl?" Gwen asked. She didn't care about the sex of the child as long as it came out normal, with no defects.

Robert paused, and his smile grew wider. "A girl to dote on. That sounds interesting."

The cork made a pop as Robert opened the bottle. He reached for Leah's glass, and she stopped him.

"Are you okay?" Robert asked.

"Just a headache. I should go lie down," Leah said with a grimace.

Gwen rolled her eyes as the woman took her time getting up. Normally, Robert would escort Leah to her room, but this time, the woman made the walk alone with slumped shoulders while Robert showered his attention on Gwen.

He placed his hand on her stomach, and she giggled. "It's too early for the baby to start kicking."

"I know. It just feels incredible. What did the doctor say?"

"I'm two weeks pregnant. I should be back in a few weeks, and then we'll have an ultrasound. But I'm healthy, and he suggested some vitamins. I'm not supposed to be stressed," she added with a pointed look.

"You won't be." Robert nodded with assurance.

She owed Trina big-time. That woman knew a couple of things about men. Although Gwen was still skeptical about her, after all, she had come from a dirt-poor background; she kind of liked her. Trina was tough and didn't let anyone get in her way. Look at how she'd come up with a great plan to get their jewelry back. Gwen didn't have any poor friends, but Trina could be the first.

At times, it felt like what they had done had been a dream. But she would never forget the thrill of holding that gun as they moved through the drug dealer's house. It was a memory she relived over and over. It was a rush she wanted more of. For the first time, she had felt in control. She had been scared, but she had been bold, ready to shoot anyone who interrupted their plans.

She reached for her phone and typed.

Gwen: I just told Robert and the witch that I'm pregnant.

Gabby: How did she react?

Gwen: Like she saw a ghost.

Gabby, Danielle, and Trina were the only ones Gwen had told about her suspicion; she would tell the other women sometime later.

Trina: And how did he react?

Gwen: Like a baby.

Even if Trina didn't send it, she could see the "I told you so" message hovering.

Trina: Now is the time to milk it. But rest assured, Leah will not take you being pregnant lightly.

Gwen nodded. She knew that. Leah was going to up her game and try to do something to take back control. Too bad she would fail. Leah needed to realize that there was only one queen, and that was Gwen, the wife, and sweetheart of Robert.

She was going to take advantage of this to the fullest. She was going to be the laziest and neediest pregnant woman to walk the surface of the earth. And she was going to throw the most glamorous baby shower ever! Way better than the crappy shower Alicia already had at the casino.

Trina: Have you girls heard from Danielle?

Her husband was probably home, and she was trying to tie him down with sex. She had been having more sex with Brad, which seemed to have her husband around more.

Gwen: No, she's probably bonking him right now.

Trina sent a laughing emoji, which made Gwen smile. She was doing a lot of that nowadays. She felt happy.

Danielle: We need to talk. It's urgent.

A chill instantly ran through Gwen. Something was up with Danielle. Now that she thought of it, the woman had been absent for the past week, missing outings and being offline most of the time, barely responding to messages. She even missed the last tea party, which was unusual.

Gabby: Are you okay?

Danielle: Someone's blackmailing me.

CHAPTER 12

DANIELLE

Trina, Gwen, and Gabby were at Danielle's house in less than an hour. Danielle opened the front door in a robe, her hair in a messy bun. She had been this way for days, and her state was worsening. This morning, she had looked at herself and couldn't recognize the shabby woman she saw.

The butler came around the corner, but she waved him off. She would attend to the ladies herself. She could see the questions in their eyes as she led them to her room for privacy.

With the door closed, she reached for the bottle of whiskey she had been nursing all day.

"Who is blackmailing you?" Trina asked with a frown.

"I don't know... I don't know," Danielle said as she sat on the bed. She had never felt this miserable in her life. How could this be happening? She was beginning to get her life back—her husband now showered her with love and attention—and this just had to happen.

"You need to tell us what's happening, so we can help," Trina said gently.

She stared at the three women. She didn't even know why she had texted them. She could handle this on her own. *Liar*, a voice whispered in her head. There was no way she could handle being blackmailed without it blowing up in her face. They were her friends—at least she thought so. A few months ago, they had shared a bonding moment that none of them had talked about since. But she felt she could trust them.

"Excuse me," Danielle said. She walked into her closet and reached for a box on the shelf where she kept her shoes, pulling some envelopes from it. She handed them over to Trina. "I started receiving this in the mail two weeks ago; they were all addressed to me."

Trina's eyes widened when she opened the envelope and pulled out a picture. It was of Danielle completely naked on a bed, her arms tied above her head. Her body was bare to the world, with her face captured. There was no doubt it was her, although she was younger.

Gwen whistled as she took the photo from Trina. "Damn, Danielle! I didn't know you were into this. You have a naughty side to you, huh?"

Danielle glared at her. This was no time for jokes. This was a serious matter.

Trina pulled a photo from another envelope, and it had a similar picture of her, only this time there was a dildo in her mouth. The rest of the photographs featured her naked in different positions. The last had a typewritten note that read, "You are going to have to pay if you don't want to have these pictures leaked online. Get ready. I will be in touch."

"Who took the pictures?" Gabby asked.

"I don't know." Danielle didn't want to look at them. She almost had a heart attack when the first one came. She had immediately gotten rid of the sexual photos. And then they had kept on coming, reminding her that no matter how many she got rid of, there were more photos out there.

"Wait! You don't know who took the pictures? You were with some guy, right? Or a girl?" Gwen asked.

Danielle took a deep breath. For years, she had kept this a secret, holding on to it as a mistake that would never come to light. Since then, she had made up for being tricked into taking nude photos by being good and playing by the rules. And in return, her life had been great.

"When I was seventeen, I met a guy at the Detroit country club. He was working there. He was cute and charming, and he paid me a lot of attention." She had been a chubby child with drab looks. None of the boys paid her any attention; instead, they went for her pretty friends. So, when he did, she had thrown all caution to the wind and felt like the most beautiful girl in the world. It was time for her to be treated like a princess by her knight.

"He seemed to like me and talked a lot to me. Every time I went there, he paid me attention. He would talk about how beautiful my eyes were, how he loved my hair…." He had taken advantage of her insecurities, using the right words that made her heart flutter. Because of him, she went to the club more to spend time with him.

"One day, he asked me out on a date. I was reluctant, but he was quite convincing. So, one night, I snuck out to be with him." She would never forget that night, how she had placed pillows on her bed, covering it up—it wasn't as if anyone would check on her. Then she quietly went down the stairs and left the house, her heart racing in fear that the floodlights would come on, and she would be caught. He'd picked her up a few houses away on his motorcycle, which added more allure to him. It had been surreal as the wind blew in her face while she held on tight. It had been everything she had imagined. It had been romantic. But she had no idea the turn things would soon take.

"We were supposed to go out on a date to the cinema to see a movie that had just been released. After that, we would go for dinner.

But he had forgotten something at home. I can't remember what it was. We drove to his apartment, and I sat in the living room while he looked for it. I think it was his wallet. Yes, it was. He handed me a drink, and after that, everything went dark."

"The bastard fucking drugged you!" Trina spat, her nostrils flaring.

Danielle nodded. Tears pooled in her eyes. She had trusted him so much and had been so foolish to think that a good-looking man like him liked a teenager who was battling puberty. He had been looking for a victim, and she had flung herself right into his arms.

"I don't know what happened next. I had no idea until now that he took pictures when I was out. When I came to, he was there and so was another girl. They were arguing, and I was naked. I was scared. I felt weak. The girl told me to put my clothes on and go home. She called me a slut and said she never wanted to see me near her man again. I quickly got into my clothes and left," Danielle said with tears rolling down her face.

"Did he rape you?" Gwen asked in a whisper.

"He didn't," Danielle said, and the women relaxed with relief. It had also been a relief to her. It would have broken her completely if he had. She had a theory he would have done so if that girl hadn't interrupted.

"How did you get home?" Trina asked.

"I had my purse with me, so I got a cab back home and snuck back in." All this had happened in about three hours. She had left an eager and excited girl and had returned devastated and in tears. She had spent hours in the tub, scrubbing her body, removing what she believed were traces of him. As the water sprayed her skin, she cried, berating herself for being naive. She should have known that no good-looking man would go for someone like her without it being a scam. That had been the lowest point in her life, and it hurt to relive it years later.

Arms wrapped around her as she sobbed loudly.

"It's going to be okay, Danielle. Just take a deep breath." Gabby comforted her.

She did as the woman instructed, taking deep breaths. "I... I didn't tell anyone what had happened. No one." The right thing to do back then would have been to tell her parents, but if she had done so, it would have backfired. Her parents had always treated her with disaffection. She was the child with the dull looks. The introverted child. The child with the average grades. Even if they had never admitted it, Danielle had been their least favorite, and they had been glad when Brad took her off their hands.

That was the only time Danielle had been helpful to them in scoring a merger with Brad's family, and she had only come in handy because her older siblings were married. "My parents would have been angry and disappointed. There had never been a scandal in the family. If I had told them, they would have sent me away. And since I wasn't raped, I felt there was nothing to report. But I couldn't stay in town and see him every time I went to the country club. So, I told my parents I wanted to finish my education in France."

"Ah! That was why you left. One day you were in school, and the next in France," Gwen said.

Danielle had left the country within a week of the incident, scared of what could happen if she stayed. For about a year, she had lived with fear, expecting the worst, that he would tell people what had happened, and she would be publicly embarrassed. Nothing happened after a while, so she returned to the US after high school.

"This is crazy. How can someone be so cruel to do such a horrible thing? First, he drugged you, and now he's blackmailing you?" Gabby said.

"This man, do you remember his name?" Trina asked.

"His name was Frank. All he gave me was the first name. I don't know if you remember him," she said to Gwen. "He used to do a lot of work at the club. The pool. The golf course. He was tall and had a beard. He told me he was twenty."

Gwen shook her head. "Sorry, I don't look at the help."

Trina shot Gwen a dirty look, but she just shrugged. "That might not have been his real name, and I m pretty sure he lied about his age as well. He was probably much older than you if he had a full beard. I doubt we'll find out anything about him at the club. A lot of time has passed. I can't help but wonder why he waited over ten years to blackmail you. He could have blackmailed you right after that. Why now? It just doesn't make any sense."

It didn't to her either. She had long forgotten the incident or had at least tried to.

"Do you think he sent the pictures to your parents and you weren't aware?" Gabby suggested.

"He didn't." She would have known. Her parents would have made sure she was aware of the mess she had gotten them into. "I don't know what I'm going to do," Danielle admitted as a fresh bout of tears emerged. "Brad is going to divorce me if he finds out. He doesn't like scandals. He won't want to be with me anymore."

"You could always explain to him what happened," Gabby suggested.

She shook her head. She knew her husband; he wouldn't understand. He was one of those men who didn't like loose women. He thought little of them. She had heard him comment about them in the past and how lucky he was to have a respectable wife. This would ruin their marriage. What would she tell her parents? They would disown her! She knew how things like this destroyed a person.

"I'm going to end up like Catherine," Danielle said.

"Who is Catherine?" Trina asked.

"Catherine used to attend our tea parties about two years ago. She had an affair, and her lover took pictures of her. They went viral, and her husband divorced her and got custody of the kids. Her family disowned her, with her father cutting her from his will. Last I heard, she was in Brazil," Gabby explained.

"Wrong information. I heard from a reliable source that she's in rehab and works as a call girl. Being a whore might not be a bad profession for you," Gwen said.

Danielle glared at the other woman, who only laughed. She didn't think this was funny at all. None of this was. Her life was practically over!

"First off, Danielle, your marriage will be all right. Frank hasn't asked for hush money yet," Trina said.

"Are you insinuating she should pay him off?" Gwen asked.

"Yes, exactly that. Pay him off. People get blackmailed all the time, and they pay. That seems like the sensible way out. It should be normal for people like you, with all your secrets and skeletons," Trina said.

"First of all, I don't know the people you know, but I don't have any skeletons. Unlike you, I'm clean!" Gwen defended.

"Pfff."

"Blackmailers tend to come back for more," Gabby added.

"I know, but we ain't sure of that. Is it a risk you are willing to take? Pay him off and move on?" Trina asked.

"But I'm going to live knowing that he's out there and may come back," Danielle said. His intention might be to turn her into a cash cow.

"The other option is to go to the cops," Trina said.

Danielle shook her head. "That would be a stupid move, and you know it. It would blow up in my face, and everyone would know what's happening."

"Fine. Then let's wait for the bastard to reach out to you and ask for money. Then we figure out our next move," Trina said.

The ladies tried to ease Danielle, and she calmed down for a bit, although all she could think of was the envelopes in her closet. She wished she hadn't been so naive years ago. Then she would not be in this mess. Because of one wrong decision, her life might as well be ruined.

They left a couple of hours later before Brad returned from work, and she promised to update them if anything happened.

Brad met her in a composed state, her bathrobe gone, her hair neat, with her makeup done. She couldn't let him see her looking untidy.

He reached for her, planting a kiss on her lips. "I brought you flowers."

Danielle noticed the fresh roses in his hand. He had been such a darling since she'd started taking Trina's advice. The way he explored her body made her flush. She had never thought she was capable of such responses.

"Are you okay? You seem tired," Brad said as he shrugged off his coat.

"My friends were over, and entertaining can be quite tiring." Danielle covered a fake yawn.

"Does that include the black woman?"

She hadn't told him about Trina, so someone must have. He saw the look of surprise on her face and laughed.

"Word around is that you ladies adopted a poor black woman as a charity project," Brad said.

She choked back a laugh. Trina would be pissed if she heard this. Poor black woman?

"Yes, she was here, and her name is Trina."

He pulled her to him, his lips on her neck. She let herself go in that moment, trying to escape her reality.

The following day, another letter came. Her hands shook as she held the envelope that was addressed to her. Without opening it, she already knew who it was from.

"Anything wrong?" Brad asked.

She flashed him a smile. "Everything is fine."

Danielle went to her bedroom after Brad left, and she opened the envelope. $200,000—that was how much he was asking for in cash. And he needed it in a week.

She was worth way more than that, but she didn't have such an amount in her account. She would need to get it from Brad, and he would want to know why she needed it. She never asked for such a large amount unless it was for a charity project. However, he would ask for receipts. She grabbed her phone and relayed the message.

Danielle: This bastard wants $200,000, and I can't get it from Brad without him asking many questions.

Trina: Is there any other means you can get the money? Your folks?

Her parents might give her the money, but they would tell Brad.

Trina: You need to come up with a solid excuse to get that money from him. If not, you're screwed.

Gwen: You want her to pay her blackmailer?

Trina: For now, I think that is the way out. But if you can come up with something else, I'm down for it.

Danielle went silent. Trina was right; this was the only way to get out of this. Pay her blackmailer, hoping he would not come back for more. Because if he did, she was screwed.

CHAPTER 13

GABBY

"The Harrisons are coming over for dinner in a week," Dave informed Gabby, and she nodded absently.

"I thought we should have the duck. It was a success the last time. Are you listening to me?" Dave asked.

"Honey, I need some money."

"Of course, I'll give you money for the dinner," Dave said as if it wasn't obvious.

"Not for that. I need $50,000," Gabby said.

"Okay." Dave shrugged.

Calm settled over her. He probably thought she was going shopping, or he just didn't care.

"Thank you." She was very appreciative of this. At least she would be able to help Danielle in paying off her blackmailer. Danielle had tried to get the $200,000 from her husband for the past three days, but Brad had only given her $80,000, which he thought was going to her children's foundation.

To Danielle's relief, Gabby and the other ladies had decided to help by contributing whatever they could. With Gabby's contribution, they were at $130k. Trina had put in $20,000, which Danielle promised to pay back. She was sure the remaining money would not be any trouble for Gwen as her husband was willing to do anything for her since her pregnancy announcement. She was surprised Gwen was willing to help; she knew the woman would rather spend that money on shopping. But people were full of surprises, after all.

Gabby: Dave has given me the money.

Gwen: Robert too. You owe me a lot, Danielle.

Danielle: Thank you so much, everyone. I promise to pay it back.

Gabby wasn't worried about her paying her back. She suspected it wouldn't be easy for Danielle to get the money without Brad being suspicious, so she wasn't expecting any of it back. It was a gift. Danielle didn't have a lot of support, and Gabby was glad to be of help.

Trina: Any news from him since?

Danielle: No. The week should be over tomorrow, so he should reach out to me. I just can't wait for this ordeal to be over.

Gabby pitied her. Danielle was a nice person and didn't deserve what was happening to her. She shuddered to think of someone blackmailing her, especially with her past. The knowledge that she had been a stripper was not hidden, but it could be embarrassing if someone tried to put it out there. She hoped the blackmailer would leave for good because it would be trouble if he returned with more demands.

Trina, Gabby, and Gwen went to Danielle's a few days later. She had gotten another message from the blackmailer. Gabby was pissed that the bastard was messing with poor Danielle. He deserved to be behind bars. But even to her, going to the cops was a stupid move. They wouldn't be able to keep a lid on it, and everyone would know what was happening with Danielle.

"I got this," Danielle said, shaking as she handed the envelope to Trina.

"Tomorrow, noon. Put the money in an unlocked black briefcase. Drive to Belle Isle Park in Detroit. Go to the lower level of the white marble water fountain, and there you will find a note. Follow the instructions. Come alone. If you try anything stupid, your pictures will be all over the internet," Trina read aloud. "I hate this dude a lot," she added.

She was not alone. Gabby disliked people like him who tried to play a fast one instead of working legitimately.

"Are you sure you want to do this?" Gabby asked Danielle, who had gone pale.

"Do I have an option?" Danielle asked quietly.

The truth was she didn't. She just had to give into the blackmailer's demands. In this case, there was not even room for negotiation.

"The truth is, you cannot go alone. We need to go with you in case something goes wrong," Trina said.

"What could go wrong?" Danielle asked, her eyes wide with fear.

"Ummm... I don't know, but anything could go wrong. And if it does, we'll dive right in and make sure you're safe," Trina said.

Gabby nodded in agreement. In movies, some blackmail scenes could turn violent, with someone getting hurt. They couldn't let Danielle go there alone. They had to watch her back.

"But he said I shouldn't come with anyone."

Gwen rolled her eyes. "I think he meant the police; besides, he won't know we're there."

"Okay. I just don't want to mess this up. I don't want him to get angry and release those pictures," Danielle said.

"Everything will go according to plan," Trina said in a firm voice that made Gabby give her a look. The woman was up to something.

"What are you up to?" she asked once the trio stepped out of Danielle's house.

"I have a feeling the asshole is going to strike again." Trina shrugged.

"And you want us to pay him off?" Gwen glared.

"What are we supposed to do?" Gabby threw back.

"Right now, we know nothing about him. We're literally under his control. We have to do whatever he says. But we need to change that. We need to find out who this man is, so if he comes back for more, we're gonna make him wish he wasn't born!" Trina said.

"So, what's the plan?" Gabby asked.

"First, Danielle can't know. You know how she'd react. She'd get fidgety, and the Frank dude will probably know she's not alone."

Trina was right about that.

"You two are going to surveil her as she goes into the park. I'm going to get there ahead of you guys and watch out for the punk," Trina concluded with a smile.

"At least this plan is not as crazy as our last one," Gabby said as Trina lifted a brow. It wasn't as crazy as what they had pulled the last time—lacing pizza with sleepy pills, entering Blu's house with guns, taking back their jewelry, and more. But somehow, this made sense. They needed to know who was behind this blackmail.

"We'll meet at the park at ten. I'll bring the guns," Trina said.

"Guns?"

Was it just her, or did Gwen light up at the word? She seemed excited like she was looking forward to tomorrow. Perhaps she'd kind of forgotten she was pregnant now.

"We need protection, don't we?" Trina said before getting into her car.

The following morning, Gabby picked Gwen up from her house. She waved to Robert as he kissed Gwen goodbye.

"So, how's Leah?" Gabby asked as she got into the car.

Gwen growled. "You just had to ruin my mood with that nasty name. The bitch is calm. Too calm. She acts all happy, but if eyes were bullets, I would be dead. Hmm. I know she's up to something, though."

"Just be careful. Some people can be dangerous," Gabby warned. She was glad she didn't have an ex-wife trying to ruin her marriage.

The ride to the park was quiet, and Gabby anticipated what they were about to do. It was a simple plan, but they needed to be discreet because the blackmailer could be watching. And if he spotted them, things could go awry. They were both dressed in simple clothes—T-shirts and leggings—and they had left their jewelry at home. The goal was to fit in.

"What if he's not alone?" Gabby wondered aloud. "These things usually involve more than one person."

"I don't know about that. I think he's some perv who spends all day watching porn. He might not have friends. He's probably ugly, and no woman wants him," Gwen spat.

"Danielle did say he was good-looking," Gabby pointed out.

"You trust young Danielle? She probably thought he walked on water."

"Don't tell me you blame her for what happened?"

"No, I don't. I blame her parents, though. She's too naive. Like a baby. But then, we all did stupid things as teenagers." Gwen smiled with a thoughtful look.

Gabby stopped the car in front of some trees, and Gwen rolled her window down. Trina emerged from the trees and pushed a black backpack through the window. It contained guns and the earphones they would use for communication.

"Keep in touch with Danielle. And don't lose sight of her. I'll be looking out for him," Trina said.

"Well…." Gabby turned to Gwen. It was time.

They waited for about an hour until they got a call from Danielle. She had arrived at the park. They watched as her car drove past them, and they followed. It was a Wednesday morning, and the park was empty except for nannies looking after children and a few oddballs.

When Danielle got out of her car, Gwen and Gabby followed on foot. It was easy to spot her. She was dressed in all black with dark sunglasses, holding a black briefcase. Gabby held back a giggle; as tense as the situation was, she was amused. It felt like a spy movie, and they were tailing a suspect.

Discreetly, they followed Danielle, pausing before taking the turns she took. The park was quiet, and Gabby's heart raced fast as they drew closer to the fountain.

Gwen pulled her back into the trees as Danielle got to the water fountain. She was the only adult there, with a few kids playing around.

"Trina, are you there?" Gwen whispered.

"I'm here, girls. Any report?" Trina's firm voice came over the earphone.

"We're at the fountain. Danielle is reaching for a note on the lower level of the marble. It's inside a waterproof bag. She's reading it now," Gabby informed. She was curious to know the details, but they couldn't communicate with Danielle, as the blackmailer could be watching.

"She's on the move," Gwen reported.

They followed her, taking cover amongst the trees. The path was quieter and more deserted, and Gabby hoped they wouldn't have to use the guns. It was one thing to use their guns in a drug dealer's crib, but out here in the open with children, they could accidentally shoot the kids and draw unnecessary attention. Then Danielle stopped in front of a row of wooden benches. She took a step, then another, ten in total, before dropping the briefcase on one of the benches. Then she turned around and headed in their direction.

"She has dropped the case and is headed back," Gabby whispered.

"Meet up with her," Trina instructed.

"What about the money!" Gwen hissed.

"Don't worry about it. Just ensure she gets back home safe. I'll meet up with you soon," Trina said.

Hiding behind the trees, they headed back the way they had come. Gabby sent Danielle a text letting her know they were on her tail and would head home together.

Twice, Danielle pulled over on the side of the road, shaking and crying. Gabby was worried, so she decided to get out of her car and ride in Danielle's car with her. She had to give it to Danielle, though she had been brave with how fragile she was. The second time she pulled over, Gabby insisted on driving. Danielle agreed, and she trembled in the passenger's seat for the rest of the ride home.

"Welcome home, ma'am," the butler said as the door opened.

Danielle ignored him, hurrying upstairs. Gabby flashed the man an apologetic smile. "She's had a long day."

He gave her a look. It wasn't even two in the afternoon yet.

Gabby found Danielle nursing a glass of whiskey. She looked tired and had bags under her eyes.

"I'm sorry you had to go through that," Gabby apologized.

"I… I was so scared. I didn't know what he was going to do. If he was going to kill me or do something," Danielle sobbed.

"What did the message at the fountain say?" Gwen asked, closing the door behind her.

Danielle handed her the paper that was on her bed. It just detailed the next steps she should take. *Head toward the benches, and after ten steps, drop the briefcase on the nearest bench.* And then a *Thank you. It was nice doing business with you.*

"Punk!" Gwen swore.

"It's over, Danielle," Gabby said, hoping she was right.

They waited for over an hour, nursing drinks and eating scones on the patio before Trina arrived, her back Sedan pulling up next to their flashy cars. Gabby smiled as Trina emerged. The way she carried herself was unique—a confident manner that yelled, "Don't fuck with me!"

The butler led Trina to the patio, and she poured a healthy amount of vodka for herself.

Gabby giggled. There were leaves stuck in Trina's hair and clothes. The laughter spread around, and soon Danielle was laughing.

"Yeah, laugh at me. You owe me, Danielle. I had to climb a tree. I battled for a spot with a squirrel," Trina said.

"Please tell me you got him," Gabby said.

Trina nodded, and Gabby relaxed. This was good news.

"You got who?" Danielle asked.

"Frank, he was working alone, which is good. Two can be quite a crowd to deal with." Trina pulled her phone from her bag and handed it to Danielle, and the others peeped in.

Trina had captured him. A skinny man with a cap over his head, holding a black briefcase.

"He's the one, right?" Trina asked.

"Umm… I don't know. It's teen years. He was bigger than this, but who knows? The cap hides his face," Danielle said.

"Swipe left. He removed his cap when he got to his car."

A few pictures later, they got a glimpse of the asshole's face. He had a thin face with big eyes and long, black, curly hair. Those eyes unnerved Gabby. He was a pervert.

Danielle shook her head. "That's not him."

"What? Come on! He was the one who picked up the briefcase." Trina groaned. "They were working as a team then. The Frank dude probably watched her to ensure she was alone while this one went for the briefcase. Shit."

The women had been quiet, staring at the picture on the phone, until Gwen suddenly announced, "I've seen that face before. I can't remember where."

"Think, Gwen! This is important!" Gabby said.

Gwen glared at her. "Don't push me. I can't recall where I've seen him right now, but it'll come to me."

"Maybe it's just your imagination," Gabby suggested.

"Nope, I've seen him before. Not worthy enough for me to remember him, but he's quite familiar."

"I got his vehicle's plate number, but I have a feeling it'll be a dead end," Trina surmised. "His car looked like a rental."

"What does this mean for me?" Danielle asked with a faraway look.

"The truth is we can't tell for now. Let's hope that all of this is over," Trina said.

Gabby hoped that this ordeal for Danielle was over and she could get her life back on track.

CHAPTER 14

TRINA

It seemed fitting for today's tea party to be held here at the country club. The sky was dull, bringing with it a cool breeze. Trina, Gwen, Danielle, and Gabby had not all attended the parties together in months, which was unusual. The women chatted in groups, talking about a wedding taking place in a few weeks. It was reported to be a merger of two powerful families.

Trina sipped her vodka settled comfortably in a lounge chair. She'd had a hectic week, and this was her way to unwind. Her phone buzzed, and she reached for it, seeing it was her cousin calling.

"Excuse me," Trina said, getting up. She headed back into the main building, toward a quiet area she had noticed when she had arrived.

"Hello, Jada."

"Where you at?" Jada asked, popping gum in that annoying way that made Trina want to snatch it from her mouth.

"You at my house?"

"Nah, but I wanna come around with Tristan. Remember him?"

Yeah, she remembered Tristan. He was her cousin's friend who had the hots for her. Tristan was dripping gorgeous with those muscular arms and cute lips, but he was a bum. He was the type of man that Trina would end up paying all his bills if they got together. The type who wouldn't work but wanted to be treated like a king. He slept all day, depending on the women in his life's ability to take care of all his needs. For her, his looks weren't enough. Trina's man needed to bring something to the table. She hadn't been born to slave her ass over some lazy guy, but she kind of missed her ex-boyfriend, Errol.

She had been in brief relationships with no serious candidate the past months. It seemed the men in the dating market had gotten even worse.

"I ain't around," Trina said.

"Don't tell me you at those rich billionaire chicks' things? You still going to that? You not tired of those bitches yet!" Jada cackled.

Trina smiled to herself.

"Guess we gonna catch you some other time. You gonna find yourself a rich white husband, right?"

"Catch you later," Trina said.

Her cousin's comment about a rich white husband had stirred some thoughts. First, she wasn't in the market for some rich white husband, but the times she came here, she could feel admiring gazes on her. If she did want a rich white husband, she could get one. It wouldn't be to be a challenge.

"Don't make me hit you!" a voice hissed from down the hall.

Her brow lifted. Quietly, she followed the voice and stopped in a hallway. There were only two people—Lori and a man she hadn't seen before. He was tall and bulky and wore a mean look. He held Lori's arm tight as he glared at her. Looking frightened, Lori lowered her face to avoid being hit.

"I'm sorry, Greg. I'm sorry. I… You weren't home when I left, and I—"

"I don't give a hoot if I wasn't around! Every time you leave the house, you will inform me. Understand?"

So, this was Lori's husband. Interesting. There were rumors about her husband being abusive to her. Shortly before Trina's call, the woman had excused herself from the tea party.

He let go of her arm and then pushed her. Trina's eyes narrowed as Lori fell to the floor, sobbing. Trina quickly moved away, hurrying to the reception. In a few seconds, the man walked past her, joining a group of men. He settled into a couch and lifted a half-filled glass, wearing a broad smile like he hadn't been abusing his wife just a moment ago.

"Lori, dear!" Trina said, wrapping an arm around the woman's waist as she knelt beside her.

Lori froze in surprise. Her eyes were red, and although she wore a long-sleeved blouse, Trina spotted the red bruises on her wrist. She scowled in the direction of her husband. Bastard! As much as Trina had wanted to intervene, she quelled the urge to rush over there and punch him in the face. Her rage would not help the situation. It would probably get her thrown out, and he would take it out on Lori when they got home.

"Ummm… Trina, what are you doing here?"

"I came to take a call. Are you okay?"

"Yeah, something got in my eye. Why don't we return to the party?" Lori asked with a smile.

She discreetly watched the woman as she returned to the party. She had suspected the rumors were true with how heavy her makeup was and the excuses she was willing to tell everyone. It was the same old story, the wife trying to protect her husband while he hurt her. She felt the utmost pity for her. Trina had once been in an abusive relationship when she was much younger and had walked out before he killed her. She shuddered to think of what she could have done to him when she realized the degree of his abuse. Thank goodness she had the nerve to walk away with what was left of her pride and not in handcuffs. And then there had been a few assholes after him who had thought they could hit her, but that never ended well for them.

Lori was a mouse, and Trina was sure it was because of her husband's oppression. Women who were abused to such an extent tended to lose their identities. She would like to help her snap out of that submissive phase, but she knew Lori had a long journey ahead of her. Women like her needed time to get out of abusive relationships, especially when married to wealthy men.

"Are you okay?" Gabby leaned forward to ask.

"Later," she said.

Gabby nodded in understanding.

After the party, they headed to a small restaurant that had become a regular to the four of them. Except, today, Danielle had to go home. She had been quite moody since they paid off the blackmailer. She lived with the fear he would return with more demands.

Over dinner, Trina told the other women what she had seen happen between Lori and her husband.

"It's no secret that he beats her, but she stays. I don't know why she doesn't just leave," Gabby said.

"Leave to where?" Gwen asked, taking a sip from her sparkling water. "She has nowhere to go, so she might as well endure."

"Gwen!"

"What?"

"So, if Robert were hitting you, you would stay?"

"First, I'm a jewel, and no one can ever hit me. But… I don't know because he treats me like the princess I am." She glared at Gabby. "Why did you even ask me that question?"

"Why did you say she has nowhere to go?" Trina asked. Women always thought there was nowhere to go, but they always had a choice—some just weren't willing or mentally strong enough to leave.

"Her father was some hedge fund manager, and he ripped his clients off and went into debt. The family estate was sold off. Her mother, a gold digger with her horrible hats, divorced him. I heard she's with a young stud in France. Many debtors came knocking on the door, and Greg—who was her father's colleague—stepped in and pumped some money to z. She came as a payment or something like that for Greg saving the day. Her father received a small settlement and lives in the Bahamas. Her siblings live off her husband's wealth. Leeches, I tell you," Gwen said.

"So, everyone gets to live a grand life while she has to make the sacrifice?" Trina asked with distaste. It never ceased to amaze her the sacrifices these women made in one way or another for their family for actions they were not responsible for. They were used as pawns, gifts, and barters.

"Trina, you're barking up the wrong tree. She's never going to leave that man," Gwen said. "Hey, you!" she yelled at a passing waiter and lifted her glass for a refill.

"When she wants to leave, she will leave," Gabby said.

How long would that take? Or would she end up in a body bag, as most extreme cases ended?

"By the way, have you recalled where you saw the man in the pictures?" Trina asked.

Gwen shook her head and handed her empty plate of crepes to the waiter. "More!" she snapped.

A pregnant Gwen was going to be more of a terror. Trina was glad she spent only a few hours with her.

It irked her that they didn't know the man's identity who picked up the briefcase. It meant unfinished business. Danielle was 100 percent sure it was not Frank, the man who had taken the pictures.

She had a bad feeling about this, that he would return. Trina was tempted to give his picture to a cop friend of hers, but he would demand many answers. Besides, getting favors from Victor came with a heavy price.

The following day was a busy day for Trina. There were a lot of customers coming in, some to buy clothes and some to use the coworking space that came with Wi-Fi and coffee. It was an idea that had popped up years ago—creating a place for freelancers and other businesspeople to meet without a formal office. It had been a hit! And she now offered subscription packages.

"Trina."

She smiled at that deep voice. Charles had his office under repair, which meant he had been around for the past three weeks. He was gorgeous, with dreadlocks and a full beard. And those firm arms of his! He was a walking, dripping chocolate ice cream. And he knew it! Whenever he walked in, several pairs of eyes followed him.

"You are gorgeous today, as always." Charles grinned.

"You got rhythm, Charles," she flirted back.

He laughed, flashing his pearly white teeth. "What are you doing this Saturday night? You wanna go out on a date with me?"

She handed him her phone. "Put in your digits. Now, you better have a fancy place to take me on Saturday."

Charles grinned. "Definitely."

As she watched his fine ass walk away, she bit her lip in excitement. She had been too busy the past few weeks with work and Danielle's troubles, but it was time for her to have some fun. Perhaps, Charles was just what she needed.

CHAPTER 15

GWEN & DANIELLE

"This tastes like garbage!" Gwen spat the pot roast back onto the plate, glaring at the waiter.

"No, ma'am! That is the best roast we have in the house tonight!" the waiter, a smallish man, defended.

Gwen's glare intensified. "And I'm telling you it tastes like rubber!"

His eyes flared as he attempted to defend himself more.

"Why don't you have something else brought to us?" Robert said calmly. He turned to Gwen.

"A pie would do. Pecan pie." Gwen shrugged.

"I thought you didn't like pie?" Jeremiah said.

She was on a double date with Robert and his old friends, Jeremiah, and Sandra Harry. She didn't like them, and the feeling was mutual, although Sandra was more of a bitch with her unsworn loyalty to Leah.

Gwen hated pecan pie on a normal day and had once flung a plate in the butler's face. But her pregnancy was giving her weird cravings. And the latest was her love for pecans, which she once disliked.

Robert smiled, placing his arm around her. "Gwen has new cravings. You see, she's pregnant."

The table went quiet; then Jeremiah clapped in excitement. "This is good news! Congratulations!"

Gwen noticed Sandra wore a look of disinterest. She was pretty sure Leah had shared the news with her and her husband, but Jeremiah was a good actor. She would rather not be here with the pretenders, but Robert had wanted her to tag along with him so he could share the news. It had been a great delight to wave to Leah as they left her behind.

The woman was beginning to fade out of their lives. Lately, she hadn't garnered Robert's attention, and he barely spared her any thought. It used to be the moment Leah called for him; he would leave whatever he was doing to be with her. He was such a baby, twisted around her finger. But not now; those days were over.

"Aren't you happy for us, Sandra?" Gwen asked.

"I am. Are you sure you want to be a mother? It takes a lot of patience to be one, and we both know you don't have any."

Like Sandra knew how to be a mother with her two stuck-up children who had their heads buried in books and nothing else. It wasn't as if they were ever going to win some nerd award or whatever they called them.

"There's always a starting point," Gwen said, lifting her glass of water in a toast. And then the glass hit the floor as a memory flooded her.

"Are you okay?" Robert asked, reaching for her.

"Yes. Just… just a little drowsy," Gwen said.

"Do you want us to return home?" Robert asked, sounding concerned.

"No… no, I'm okay. I just need to use the restroom." She stepped over the shards, then hurried off.

As she'd lifted her glass, she recalled where she had seen Danielle's blackmailer. That face had been haunting her for weeks as she'd tried to figure out the mystery.

Shortly after she entered the ladies' room, the door opened, and Sandra walked in with crossed arms. "Robert asked that I follow you. I'm sure that was one of your little games to get attention," the older woman sneered.

Gwen rolled her eyes. Sandra had such an annoying voice, like Leah. She pulled her phone out of her purse and began to type, the woman's gaze on her.

Gwen: I know where I saw that perv.

Gabby: Where?

Gwen: At the casino. I'm on a date with Robert and his loony friends. I'll share the details later.

"You're stupid if you think having a baby will tie Robert down," Sandra said.

Gwen looked up. She had forgotten the woman was even there. "Sandra, why don't you tell Leah to give it up? She lost. It's time for her to move on." And with that, she walked past Sandra with a broad smile.

Later in bed, with Robert fast asleep, Gwen reached out to the other ladies and gave them the full details.

Gabby: Where have you been, Gwen?? You can't just leave us hanging.

Gwen: I have more important things to do, you know.

Trina: Dinner with Robert and his loony friends?

Gwen: As I said, he was at Alicia's baby shower at the casino. I remember seeing him from across the room. He was looking at us like a creep.

It had been unusual the way he continued staring at them, and at one point, she'd suspected he had a sight problem—one of those freaks who wasn't staring at you, but their eyes were on you.

Trina: Was he gambling there?

She rolled her eyes. Someone like him didn't have the money to play at such an expensive place.

Gwen: He worked there. He had on the help uniform.

Trina: The help uniform?

Danielle: She means the black-and-white outfit.

Trina: Gwen, you never cease to amaze me.

Gwen: I have no idea what that means, and I don't care. He was working a couple of tables. I assumed it was the first time he had seen wealthy women in his life. There were a lot of call girls there with fake fur and cheap perfume.

Trina: Of course.

Gwen: And somewhere in the night, I forgot about him. People like that are not important.

Gabby: Danielle, when did the first note come?

Danielle: Three days after the shower.

Gabby: I think seeing you at the shower triggered the note.

Trina: I think Gabby is right. All these years and nothing happened until after the shower. Are you sure you don't know who he is? He doesn't look familiar in any way?

Danielle: I don't know that man.

Trina: At least we have a trace on him.

Gwen: It might be a dead end. If he were smart, which I doubt he is, he would have quit his job and left town.

Trina: Not everyone's as smart as you, Gwen.

Gwen scowled. Why did that feel like an insult and a compliment at the same time?

DANIELLE

The ladies were at Trina's home, a long way from theirs. Despite what had happened months ago, they still had the courage to come around. While munching loudly, Gwen nursed a plateful of peanuts, which she allowed no one to share.

"It is up to you, Danielle," Trina said.

Danielle sighed. It was a difficult decision for her to make. "But what if he doesn't come back?"

"And what if he does? I feel bad that he'll be back soon, and when he returns, we need to be prepared," Trina said.

It wasn't easy acting like everything was okay, and Brad could see right through her. She wanted all of this to be over. She was scared that if they investigated her blackmailer, he would retaliate and ruin her life. Wasn't it better to let sleeping dogs lie? But Trina had a point. What if he returned? She couldn't continue paying a blackmailer over and over. Where would she get the money from?

"You make the call, Danielle," Gabby said.

"I… Fine! Let's do this. But we need to be as discreet as possible, please. I don't want to piss him off," Danielle said, not believing she would do this.

"We won't. We'll be as discreet as possible. If he begins to suspect, we'll back out as soon as possible," Trina assured.

Danielle hoped she wasn't making a mistake. The truth was, she was confused about which decision to make.

"The best place to look for him is at the casino. Gwen, you and I will head there tomorrow," Trina said.

Gwen froze. "Go with Gabby. I have things to do."

"What things?"

"I'm pregnant!" Gwen whined, pointing at her stomach.

"You are a great distraction, Gwen. Tomorrow, you will be my plus-two." Trina laughed.

Gwen glared at her. "You don't know how to treat a pregnant woman. First, be kind to me."

"Right," Gabby mumbled, earning a laugh from Danielle.

"Thank you for doing this," Danielle said with seriousness. Her life over the past few weeks had been depressing. She was a shadow of herself. She had a lot to lose if those pictures came out in public. Worse, she'd had no bargaining power; her blackmailer had controlled their transaction, leaving things one-sided, so she had no assurance that it was over. Someone out there still had pictures of her naked, and they could do whatever they wanted with them.

"How was your date last night?" Gabby asked.

Trina grinned. "It went well. He was a gentleman all through."

"Did you guys do it?" Gwen smiled.

"What are you? Twelve? And no, we didn't. It's frustrating, you know. I just want to jump on him. But he wants things to go slow. I love slow, but not that slow." Trina took a long sip from her glass.

"Then why not jump on him?" Danielle wondered aloud.

"I want him to feel in control. If I jump on him, he may think little of me, so I will let him go at his own pace. For now. It'll get to a stage where I have to take the reins."

Danielle envied Trina. She wished she could take the reins of her life. If Trina had been blackmailed, Danielle was sure Trina wouldn't have paid a cent. She would have given the blackmailer a "fuck you" sign and laughed it off. Or tracked him down and kicked his ass. But she wasn't Trina. She was a woman who had a lot at stake if her past was revealed. And if she went down, she might never recover from it.

She returned to a quiet house. Brad had gone on one of his trips, and truth be told, she wanted the space. It was a mystery how she hadn't broken down and told him all that had been happening because it was right on the tip of her tongue. But the fear of what he would do scared her. She had been acting frigid these past few days, and she hoped his time away would help her resolve the issue at hand, so by the time he returned, she would be back to her cheery self.

Her mother-in-law dropped by shortly after she got home. She wasn't in the mood for socializing, but courtesy demanded that she attend to her.

"Where's Brad?" Martha asked, pulling away from their hug.

"He went on a trip."

"You look pale. And thin."

"I have been busy lately."

"With the tea party? I've been hearing a lot about it. It seems rather interesting. I should drop by some afternoon," Martha said, taking a teacup from the butler.

Danielle held back a laugh. She would certainly be shocked, especially if Trina was going to teach them a new way to get a hold of their marriages.

"How is Cindy?" she asked, referring to her sister-in-law.

"She's in Italy for a job. A beautiful place with history. You should go there sometime."

As the woman droned on, Danielle realized it had been a while since she had last gone on a vacation. Brad was always too busy, and he didn't want her to go off on her own. She needed a break from this drama and a change of scenery. When he returned, she would convince him to go on a trip. Perhaps for a month or two. And if he weren't free, she would have to go on her own.

She got out of bed early the next day and headed to the studio for a Pilates session. Her attention was barely there as she thought of the investigation Trina and Gwen were going on. She hoped they returned with some good news. What she would do with that news, she wasn't sure of. It wasn't as if she could go to the police and tell them that she had been blackmailed. Besides, Frank and his accomplice could be long gone by now.

Her phone buzzed at noon. It was Trina.

Trina: We just left the casino. We spoke to a few employees. I showed one or two his picture, and they told me his name is Matt Posser.

Gwen: He's such a creep. He has no friends, and no one knows where he lives.

Trina: He's a loser.

Gwen: I would say a sociopath.

Trina: He stopped working there two weeks ago. He called in, saying that he quit, and no one has seen him since then.

Gabby: Did you get his number?

Trina: Yes, we did. But the service provider said his number was unreachable. I bet he's gotten rid of the SIM card so that no one can get through to him.

Gwen: We can still find him. All we need to do is pay a nerd, and we will have his address by nightfall. Or we get his fingerprints and get his personal information.

Gabby: Gwen, we are not the CIA. And where would we get a hacker? You don't find them playing around.

Trina: Having a name is enough to get more information if the need arises. We all have internet footprints, and we can find him no matter what. But we don't need to worry, right? He might be on some island right now.

Danielle: Thank you. I feel much better now that we know who he is.

Matt Prosser. That was the asshole who had blackmailed her. She had a feeling she would sleep better that night.

CHAPTER 16

GWEN, TRINA, DANIELLE & GABBY

Leah was sick, or so she claimed. Over breakfast, she had just told Robert that she had found a lump in her breast as Gwen talked about going to the hospital with him in a few days for an ultrasound.

"A lump? That could be…." Robert had gone pale.

Leah nodded. "I don't know what to think, Robert. I'm scared."

Gwen frowned as her husband let go of her hand and went around the table to hug the witch. What on earth was this woman still doing in her home? She had a loft and a country home, but she chose to disrupt their lives with her presence.

Gwen could see right through her lies. Did Leah have cancer? Hell no, miserable people like her lived long. It showed how crazy Leah was to lie that she had cancer, to go to that extent. Gwen couldn't applaud her. That was low, like the slime that she was.

There was no way this woman had cancer! That meant hell if she did have it. Robert would want to be by his best friend's side 24/7.

"You should have that checked," Gwen said.

"My appointment is in two weeks, and I'm so scared. You'll be with me, right, Robert?" Leah asked, holding his hand.

He nodded. "Yes, I'll be with you. I'm going to have the best doctors care for you."

"And if you die, we'll name our next child Leah." Gwen smiled, her hand going to her bump.

Leah went pale as Robert shot her a look. She shrugged. What? Leah should be honored that she would name her daughter after her even if it were a promise she would never fulfill. No child of hers deserved such a horrible name.

"Why don't we go for a walk? It should cheer you up," Robert said.

"Yes, we should. I feel choked up here," Leah said, retaking Robert's hand.

Gwen's eyes remained pinned on them as they walked away, arm in arm. That act hadn't fooled her. She wasn't going to get Robert's attention by claiming she was sick. Cancer indeed!

She felt a stir in her stomach. It was probably gas because Gwen was just in her second trimester. Being pregnant was certainly not easy. She hoped she wouldn't swell or puke like most women did. So far, it had been an easy ride. She did have certain cravings, and she was less pissed nowadays and more patient—although she was quite needy and wanted to be catered to all the time. Robert had gotten her a personal assistant to do her every wish, some skinny dude who she suspected was gay. He could be quite yappy, but he knew fashion and had several connections to luxury brands. So, she guessed she didn't mind him sticking around for now.

Her phone buzzed, and she groaned as she stared at the message.

Danielle: He's back again.

She didn't have to be told who it was. That scoundrel!

Gwen: What happened this time around?

Danielle: Another letter came. He's asking for $500,000.

Gabby: That asshole is crazy. I thought he was gone.

Gwen had doubted he was gone. Paupers like him came back for more. He must have gone through the money in the past month and now wanted more.

Gwen: We need to get rid of him for good.

Gabby: Yes, we do. Because he's going to keep coming back for more. How long did he give you this time around?

Danielle: Ten days.

Gwen: How kind of him. Trina, are you there? What do we have on him so far?

Trina: To be honest, I haven't found out much. I've been too busy, and I kind of forgot. He's offline. He has a Facebook page, but the last time he made a post there was like four years ago. Or he probably deleted his recent posts.

Gwen: And Frank? Have you found a connection between them?

Trina: I was so focused on Matt that I didn't bother with him.

Gwen: We all know I'm the smart one.

Trina: I'll get back to you all.

She wondered what she would do if she were in Danielle's shoes. Tell Robert. That was what she would do. She knew he'd be able to handle the issue discreetly. Her husband might seem like a gentleman, but she knew he was ready to do anything when it came to those he loved. But she wasn't Danielle with her stuffy husband. Whatever Trina came up with, they were not paying him off this time around. They were going to get even... whatever that was.

They met three days later at Gabby's house. Danielle looked a mess like she hadn't been to the spa in weeks. Pushing Trina out of the way, Gwen settled into a recliner couch, which was good for her legs.

"Happy with yourself?"

"I am," Gwen said, taking a bowl of peanuts from Gabby. They had become her favorite, and she snacked on them all day.

"What have you found out?" Danielle said, pulling dark sunglasses from her eyes.

Gwen gasped. "You look terrible. I must give you the number to my spa. You need to get those lines and bags fixed. I understand you're going through something, but you can't just let yourself go."

Danielle turned to Trina. "Please tell me you found something. I'm going crazy! I can't do this again. I just can't."

"I did. This Matt guy is Frank's cousin. And get this, Frank is dead."

Silence descended over the room. "Wait, the Frank dude is dead?" Gabby asked.

"Yes. Lucky for us, Frank was quite popular on social media with probably thousands of pictures, most of them with women. He died a year ago in an accident. I had to go back about six years before I found any connection with Matt," Trina informed, pouring wine from a bottle into a glass.

"Now it makes sense why the blackmail came suddenly," Gabby said.

"Get this, I spoke to one of Frank's old friends. I told him I had just returned to the country and was trying to get in touch with Frank, and I heard that he was dead. I asked about his family, and he told me Frank's parents were dead and that he was not on good terms with the rest of his family. He told me that his cousin—he didn't give me his name, but it was obvious it was Matt—was the one who got his inheritance, an old house," Trina said.

"He must have found the pictures, and when he saw me in the casino…."

"He decided to use the pictures to get money out of you. A little brilliant for someone like him," Gwen said.

"I wish I hadn't gone to that shower," Danielle muttered.

"Yeah, the drinks were horrible, and I can't get that tacky dress Alicia wore out of my head." Gwen sighed.

"One way or another, he would have found you. What has happened has happened," Gabby said. She turned to Trina. "Please tell me you know where he is."

Trina smiled widely. "You know I do. Let's just say Frank's friend wasn't the smartest; he gave me Matt's address."

"So, what do we do with this now? I mean, do we just go there and ring the bell and kindly ask him to turn the pictures over?" Gabby wondered aloud.

"We could always tie him up and threaten him," Gwen offered. If they were being honest with themselves, that was the best option because the asshole didn't deserve to be treated nicely.

"I have to agree with Gwen. He's a jerk, and we need to be strict with him, but first, we need to find out if he even lived there or if he's moved out. It would be foolish of him to still live there after what he's gotten himself involved in. Why don't we go on a road trip tomorrow, ladies?" Trina suggested.

"Tomorrow is fine with me," Danielle said quickly.

"Me too," Gabby agreed.

Everyone turned to Gwen, who rolled her eyes. "I have things to do, but I can fit you all in."

"It's a date then!" Trina smiled.

Loud rap music filled the car, and Trina bopped to it. She was the driver, and she controlled the music. Period! She smiled as she caught

Gwen's irritated look from the back seat.

"How much longer will it take before we get there?" Gwen asked.

"Probably an hour more." Trina hadn't realized how far away he lived until she put the location in the GPS. The roads were getting quiet, with only a few vehicles. They would be back by nightfall.

"This is definitely like something out of a scary movie. I wonder which of us is going to survive," Gabby said with a giggle.

"Nobody is going to die," Danielle said sternly.

Trina smiled at the fear in her voice. However, she was far from scared. If anything happened, the ladies were prepared to defend themselves. They were going to scope out the territory, after which they would return home and figure out what was next. Besides, they had their weapons with them.

A few minutes later, they arrived at a small town called Battle Creek. This was a lovely community, but the city was dying, and jobs were hard to come by unless you worked at the famous Kellogg Cereal place.

The houses were scattered around, far away from the others. It took a while with some wrong turns before they located the house. It was easy to spot. A rundown house with an overgrown lawn. They parked the car behind a high hedge where they wouldn't be spotted. Then, they proceeded to wait.

"How much longer are we going to sit here? I need to use a restroom," Gwen whined.

"I asked if you wanted to take a leak at the gas station we drove past," Trina said with an eye roll.

"Never would I use a restroom in a dirty gas station. I'm sure roaches crawl around in there," Gwen snapped.

"Well, you'll just have to do your business in the bush, lady, because it might take hours before we leave."

She mumbled something Trina couldn't catch, but she felt the other woman's eyes bore into her from behind. But Gwen was kind of right. She was getting tired of waiting. It seemed Matt had moved out of there. She glanced at her watch. She was supposed to have a date with Charles tonight, but she would have to postpone, which she wasn't looking forward to. She liked Charles. He was a great guy in and out of bed, with barely any baggage. He had no crazy exes or baby-mama drama. He was smart and had a legit business. Trina wanted to keep dating him for now.

"Someone's coming!" Danielle said.

A sound came from down the road, and a shiny, red car drove into the driveway of the house.

"He bought that car with our money!" Gwen spat.

Damn right! She supposed it was a Cadillac, a new model because that was what an idiot like him would get. He was even stupid enough to come back here. He stepped out of the car, and she recognized him as the man she had seen at the park that day. He had a black briefcase with him, identical to the one Danielle had left. She froze as he turned around, surveying his environment. Not spotting them, he turned around and went to the front door, letting himself in.

"Whoa! For a moment, I thought he saw us," Gabby said, letting out a breath.

"He's the one in the picture," Danielle said, seated next to her.

"Yes, and at least we know he still lives here," Trina said.

"Now, can we go?"

"Hush, Gwen. We need to wait some more. Trina wouldn't put it past him to do so. He could be at the window watching."

"Better be fast; I can't hold on any longer. Unless you want me to go in your car, I need to pee." Gwen smiled wickedly.

Trina shuddered. She was sure Gwen would do it just for the thrill. A car came into view, and she used that opportunity to get on the road. She frowned as the car drove past them.

"Wait!" Trina yelled.

"What?" Danielle asked.

"Nothing. I thought I saw someone I know."

They talked about the next steps on the way back. They were going to break in, tie him up, and have him hand over all the pictures he had of Danielle and ensure that he never threatened Danielle again. Now that they knew where he lived, they would be well prepared.

"I think we should use the Taser," Gabby suggested.

"Or we could crack his head open with a gun," Gwen said. She had become cheerier ever since she used the restroom in a small restaurant. She rated it as average, but at least she wasn't threatening to urinate inside Trina's vehicle anymore.

"Gabby's idea seems like a good plan. We don't want to kill him; we want to make him scared and probably not skip town with any of the money he still has. Next time, he won't mess around with us," Trina said.

As they continued going over their plan, something kept tugging at her mind, something she couldn't place her finger on. She hated when this shit happened. It would haunt her until she could finally remember whatever it was.

She dropped the women off in town, and they agreed she would pick them up in two days. Then they would make their move.

It was completely dark when she got home. The headlights of her car rested on Charles, who sat at her doorstep. She groaned. She had forgotten to call for a rain check.

"I am so sorry!" Trina said, hurrying to hug him. "I was supposed to call you, but I was so occupied. How long have you been waiting?"

"Two hours. I called you, but your phone was dead."

"I apologize. Now come in and let me make it up to you." She grinned as she opened the door. He took the bag from her, the bag that contained the guns and other tools.

"So, where you been? I called your store, but you weren't there," Charles said.

"I went out with Gabby and her friends," Trina said, shrugging out of her coat.

"Still can't believe you got those snooty, rich friends. That's unlike you." Charles pulled her to him.

Trina chuckled. He knew her, but at the same time, he didn't.

CHAPTER 17

GABBY & TRINA

"**Y**ou have been doing a lot of socializing these days," Dave said.

Gabby looked up from her breakfast. "Yes, we're working on a project."

"You need any money?"

She smiled. "Yes, we do."

Dave got up from the table. "I'll send some to your account," he said before taking a sip from his teacup. "I'll be back late tonight. I have a meeting that will run late."

That was great with her, giving her enough time to get back. Last time, she had returned late and had missed dinner with him.

"Have fun," Dave said before planting a kiss on her lips.

She sure was going to have fun. After breakfast, she headed upstairs and changed into her outfit, the same one she had worn when they made the hit on Blu's crib.

A cab waited for Gabby as she emerged from the house, her eyes covered with dark sunglasses.

She was the last to arrive at a small McDonalds, Gwen glaring at her impatiently.

"Don't you know we need to leave early so we can get back sooner?" Gwen snapped.

"I am early," Gabby said. She turned to Danielle. "How are you?"

"Good. I can't wait for this to be over."

"Trina told us something strange that makes me believe she needs to get her eyes checked," Gwen said.

"Trina said she saw Greg as we left Matt's house two days ago. He was driving the car that passed by us," Danielle said.

"Greg? Which Greg are you talking about?" Gabby asked, confused.

"Lori's husband. I know it sounds unbelievable, but I'm sure it was him. I can't forget his face," Trina said.

"That is strange. I… What would Greg be doing there? Are you sure he was the one you saw? We were in a rush and trying to get away," Gabby said.

Trina frowned. "I'm pretty sure he was the one I saw. Maybe he had family around?"

"I doubt it. Greg comes from wealth, not some crumbling neighborhood. Maybe he has a tramp he visits there. She probably opens her legs for him on cornstalks."

"Gwen!"

"What?"

"Can we go?" Gabby asked with a sigh.

Trina had gotten a rental for their outing today. It was a small vehicle that had Gwen complaining as she settled into the front seat.

"Couldn't you get a bigger vehicle?" Gwen complained.

"This was the only one available on such short notice with tinted windows," Trina said as she pulled off.

Music from the radio played in the background as they went over their plan. Their plan was dependent on Matt being home. If he were home, they would use a ruse to get him out of the house while they went in. They would break in and wait for him if he wasn't home.

The ride seemed faster this time, probably because they didn't have to make wrong turns. The familiar house loomed ahead as they drove past it. The red car was in the driveway.

"Shit! He's home!" Trina said.

Like her, they had been hoping for the easy way out—break in and get him unaware.

They went down the road past the house, and Trina reversed and drove them back the way they had come, pulling quietly behind the high hedge they had hidden behind two days ago.

"So, you all know what to do, right?" Trina said as she inserted her earphones in her ears.

"Yes, we do," Danielle said.

"Good luck," Gabby said as Trina grabbed her purse that contained a Taser and gun.

Gabby knew Trina could take care of herself—she had always been tough—but she hoped things didn't go wrong because blackmailers could turn crazy. The plan seemed straight, though. Trina had not been at the baby shower so that Matt wouldn't suspect her—at least they hoped not.

Her eyes followed Trina as she went across the road, walking past the car to the front door.

She heard Trina knock on the door with the knocker through the earphones. "Hello!" Trina called.

After a few more knocks, she rang the bell.

"Hello! Please, I need help. My car broke down, and I need to use your phone!"

"What's happening?" Danielle whispered.

Gabby wondered the same too. Did he suspect something foul? If so, they needed to come up with another plan on the spot.

"Guys, the door is open," Trina said as the door creaked open.

"Trina! Get out of there! That freak is going to jump on you!" Gwen yelled.

"Stop screaming in my ears. I have my hand on my gun," Trina snapped.

"What's happening, Trina?" Gabby had a bad feeling about this. They needed to get out of there now!

"Oh my God! Fuck! Fuck!"

"Trina! What the hell is happening?" Danielle asked, reaching for the door handle.

"He's dead."

TRINA

Trina had seen a few dead bodies in her life. Her grandmother, her dad, and her cousin. But they had looked peaceful. This one was messed up. And violent. Matt's head had been bashed in over and over, and flies were circling about the remains.

The ladies rushed into the house.

"Oh my God!" Gwen went pale, holding her stomach. She was the first to spot the body, the others behind her.

"Hold that in!" Trina warned, voice steely. "You cannot leave DNA behind."

Perhaps it was the thought of being arrested for the murder of a scumbag, but Gwen gulped whatever was in her mouth back in.

"Someone killed him," Gabby whispered, her eyes trained on the body. "Who could do such a horrible thing?"

All eyes turned to Danielle, who took a step back.

"Did you hire someone to kill the fucker, Danielle?" Gwen asked.

"No! I didn't! I would never kill anyone. We had a good plan," Danielle said, shaking.

"Enough!" "I don't think Danielle did it." Trina had a feeling Danielle was going to blow up, and an exchange of words would follow.

"That's what they all say," Gwen whispered.

"And you know it too. She may have had a motive to do so, and even the capacity, but she didn't. Someone got to him before we could," Trina said, staring at the corpse.

"Gabby, check if there's another entry, and make sure you wear your gloves; we don't want to leave any trace of us behind," Trina said.

Being here, they were compromising the crime scene. They could go to jail for this. Trina shuddered at the thought. She had never imagined she would face jail time because of some spoiled, rich white women—what a way to go down.

"There's a back door!" Gabby called. Trina followed her voice into the kitchen, which had a door leading outside. It was locked.

Gabby and Trina returned to the other ladies who stood far away from the body.

"There's are two entryways. One is locked, and the other was open when I came in. There are no smashed windows. Matt probably let his killer in through the front door, they walked in together, then he made the mistake of turning around for a second, and he was struck." Trina stated before being interrupted.

Gwen clapped. "Nice one, Detective. Are you sure you didn't do the job?"

"And then someone ransacked the house," Trina continued. The chairs in the living room had been tossed, and the cushion ripped. Cupboards were pulled apart. Even the kitchen had not been spared.

"The person was looking for something."

"It could have been more than one person," Gabby added.

She was right. It could have been more, just like there were four of them.

"They have probably been blackmailed by him and were looking for their photos," Gwen said.

Exactly! She turned to the body again. Damn, had they done a number on him. If he weren't wearing the red T-shirt and black pants he had worn two days ago, Trina wouldn't have known he was the one.

"He was killed two days ago," Gabby said, reading her mind.

"How do you know?" Danielle asked.

"Same clothes," Trina answered.

"So, someone came here when we left. It could have been…." Gwen's eyes widened, and she turned to Trina. "Are you sure it was Greg you saw?"

She hadn't wanted to be the one to link Greg to this, but he had been the first person on her mind. He had the rage to do such a thing from what she knew of him.

"Greg? I know he's mean to Lori, but to do this… it seems far-fetched," Danielle defended.

Trina scoffed. A man who could hit a woman was capable of this.

Trina left the living room and pushed a door open; it revealed a bedroom with barely any furniture. The bed was removed from its frame with the drawers of a dresser tossed to the ground. He had not found what he was looking for here either.

"Find anything?"

Trina jumped, glaring at Gabby, who flashed her an apologetic smile.

"No, we need to check upstairs." She glanced at her watch. "We need to do what we have to do and leave here fast."

There were three rooms upstairs with barely any furniture, and like downstairs, it had been ransacked. The last room seemed to be the one Matt had occupied before his death. There were clothes strewn over the floor with shoes tossed around. The bathroom had grooming items inside the vanity sink, removed from an overhead cabinet.

"I don't think he found what he was looking for," Danielle said.

Yes, because he had ransacked the entire house.

"So, Matt was blackmailing Greg? I wonder what he had on him that would make him kill him so violently," Gwen wondered aloud.

It didn't even matter what it was. Greg seemed like the type of person who would kill because he liked to be in control, and someone having something to restrain that control was a flaw in his power. Men like him didn't want some lowlife punk dangling their life before them.

They headed downstairs, trading theories of what Matt had over Greg. The guy was an idiot. He should have left town with the money he got after the first blackmail. But no, he had been consumed by greed and wanted more. And he had met his death.

Did he deserve to die? Trina wasn't one to say otherwise, but it seemed death was the perfect answer to stop him. Even if they had beaten the crap out of him, what was the guarantee he wouldn't return and retaliate?

"If Greg found the pictures, then he knows about me," Danielle said, her eyes widened with fear.

"Damn! I would rather the dead guy has them than Greg. That guy is so crazy, and we have no idea what he's capable of," Gabby said.

"I have a feeling the pictures are still here, and it would not be wise to leave without them. They will be easily linked to you," Trina glanced at Danielle. If the cops found those pictures, she would be on the suspect list. They all knew what that meant.

"Where would a creep like him hide those pictures?" Gwen wondered aloud.

"Probably the same place he found them. Where Frank kept them," Gabby said.

"Let's spread out and look around for them. They were probably in an obvious place, staring at them as they looked around. Here, put these gloves on. We don't want to leave our fingerprints on anything," Trina said.

An hour later, they regrouped in the living room. They were tired, but Gwen surprised her by not complaining throughout the search.

"Nothing! I couldn't find anything," Danielle said with a sad look.

"I found these!" Gwen said, dropping three briefcases on the table.

Danielle reached for them. They were all empty. Trina was not surprised. They had probably contained money a while ago.

"Maybe we should come around another day," Danielle suggested.

Trina gave her a look. "If he didn't find what he wanted, he might return, and this time, he might find the pictures."

Hands on her waist, she looked around. Where would she hide something so that no one would find it? For the guns, she would use space under her closet. She had discovered a loose tile while cleaning and had opened it to find a large space where others must have stored their valuables in the past.

Trina's eyes narrowed as she approached the stairway. There was a dark space underneath, occupied by an old bicycle.

Trina asked Gabby to bring her cell phone over; it was the only thing she could think of that might have a light on it. She shone it over the floor and found a trapdoor. She pulled hard on it and stared into the vast darkness.

"I think we've found a basement," Trina said. The beam of the light landed on a rickety staircase. Trina went down first; it was steadier than it looked.

It was a small room and very cold, even though she could not spot any ventilation system. She flashed the light around until she found a light switch. Bright light filled the room. There was a cot with rumpled sheets, a dirty sink, and a table covered with a camera and lenses. Over the table was a bright fluorescent bulb. This had probably been his darkroom. She walked toward a shelf and reached for a file.

"I found them!" Trina yelled.

CHAPTER 18

DANIELLE, GABBY, GWEN & TRINA

Relief overwhelmed Danielle as she stared at the pictures. They had found them! She couldn't believe it. She had almost given up.

"This guy was a perv," Gabby said as she pulled a set of pictures from a folder. Danielle leaned forward. Like her, another girl lay on a bed naked, her eyes closed and her arms tied above her.

How many people had this asshole drugged and molested? She wished she hadn't been so gullible. She wouldn't be caught in any of this ever again.

"Guys," Gwen said with urgency.

Danielle hurried to her and gasped. They had thought Greg was the one who was being blackmailed. But they had been wrong. Lying on a bed naked was Lori.

"Wow!" Gabby said.

"Now, I didn't expect this. Could Lori have been the one who killed him?" Trina wondered aloud.

"Lori? She looks like she can't hurt a fly," Danielle said.

"Murderers don't have a sign on their forehead that says 'I kill people.'" Gwen rolled her eyes.

"But you saw Greg, right? Not Lori. Or could they have done it together?" Gabby asked.

"Great! They are both crazy!" Gwen said.

"We have everything we need," Trina said. They gathered all the pictures and negatives and were even fortunate enough to find some money Matt must have stashed down there. Now they could go home and get rid of the photos. Danielle was going to take delight in watching them burn to ashes.

"Let's get out of here. I'm getting the chills," Gwen said, heading for the stairs.

Danielle agreed with her. She was freaked out being down there.

"What do we do with the dead body?" Gabby asked as she reached the top of the stairs, Trina behind her. She slammed the basement door closed.

"We leave it as we saw it. We're not going to tell anyone," Trina said.

"Yes, that's right, we're not going to tell anyone." A familiar voice said from the doorway.

Danielle froze, her heart pounding in fear. She was not the only one. As the ladies entered the living room, they couldn't believe who had just entered through the front door.

Standing in front of them was Greg with a gun pointed at them.

"Greg?" Danielle squeaked.

"I see you have found the pictures. I combed the house but couldn't find them. You bimbos are good for something, I guess. Now hand them over to me. Now!" he snapped as Trina hesitated. "Drop them nice and slowly on the ground and kick them to me."

He had always unsettled her with those crazy eyes of his, but now she was freaking scared. He held a gun, and she was sure he didn't mind using it. They had their guns, but he would hurt the ladies before they could reach for them.

"I'm putting them down right now," Trina said as she lowered her body.

Everything that happened next was a flash. Trina sprung on him, but he was a big man. He shoved her to the ground, kicking her in the stomach. Trina yelped with pain.

"Stupid bitch! You couldn't just mind your business. You should be in the ghetto where you belong instead of trying to corrupt these ladies!"

"I'm not—"

"Shut up! You think I don't know the slutty things you teach them? Trying to make my wife a slut?" Greg snapped.

Trina moved out of the way before he could kick her again.

"Greg!"

With his gun pointed at Trina, his eyes turned to Gwen.

"Why don't you let me go, Greg?" She pointed at her stomach; her face wore the softest look Danielle had ever seen on her. "I'm pregnant. I'm going to be a mother. The best gift ever. Let me go, and I won't tell anyone. You can keep the rest of them."

He glared at her. "You think I'm stupid, you brat?"

"Idiot," Gwen mumbled, throwing him a pissed look.

"You bitches can't just mind your business. No, you must poke your nose into matters that don't concern you. I blame it on your weak husbands. They cannot control you."

"Like you control Lori?" Danielle said, surprised at the firmness of her voice.

"You were the one he was blackmailing, right?" Greg asked, giving her a slow, lecherous look. "You're a slut! Just like my wife, who opened her legs for that peasant!"

"I was drugged! And I'm pretty sure she was too!"

He glowered at her. "Don't make excuses, you cunt! You women are all the same. Empty heads! You have nothing to offer but that hole between your legs."

Greg had never come off as a misogynist. She'd had no idea how little he thought of women, but how much did she even know him? Not at all, she realized. There was so much bitterness in him. He was crazy!

"So, you killed Matt. You must have followed him here from the park," Trina said, taking his attention from her.

"I don't owe you an explanation, but since you're all going to die anyway, I should grant you your final wish, right?" he sneered.

"You probably found the pictures and blackmail letter in the mailbox," Gabby said.

"I open all the mail!" He fumed. "And I found those dirty pictures. Those horrible pictures of the slut I married. I confronted her, and she was like you, making excuses." He grinned. "I beat her up so bad she couldn't walk."

"Greg, put the gun down so I can beat the shit out of you. What kind of man would beat up on his wife? You are a coward," Trina yelled.

This man was crazy. Why had no one stepped in to protect Lori? Danielle shuddered to think of living with such a lunatic.

"I made her go there to drop off the briefcase, and then I followed the bastard. I followed him here and took my money back."

"You didn't even give him a chance to tell you where he kept the pictures. That's why you ransacked the house," Trina said.

His eyes narrowed on her. "Enough of the talking!" The gun pointed at her, and she squealed. "Gather together, all of you! I'm going to end this right now!"

"Greg, you don't want to do this. I'm carrying a baby, if you haven't noticed. Robert's firstborn!" Gwen pleaded as she moved behind Trina.

Trina threw her a look that told her to remain calm. Gwen saw her carefully reach for her gun, which was tucked behind her.

"You're all going to die. And no one's going to care! I'm going to—"

Just as he was completing his threat against the ladies, the gun went off, and Gwen screamed. Danielle, who stood there praying, was afraid to open her eyes. Then it went quiet. Danielle opened her eyes and gasped. Standing in front of Greg's body was Lori. Danielle jolted as three more gunshots filled the air, all targeted at Greg until his body went still.

Where the hell had she come from? Danielle wondered as her heart pounded. Today had to be the craziest day of her life.

"Put the gun down, Lori," Trina said, her gun trained on the other woman.

Lori was a mess. Her face was covered with bruises, and she had aged a decade. She dropped to the floor, her body shaking as she sobbed. Gabby went to comfort her as Trina took the gun and tucked it in her pants.

"Hey, dear, it will be okay," Gabby comforted.

"I… I killed him," Lori barely got out as she struggled to breathe, hyperventilating.

"You saved us, Lori. He would have killed us," Trina replied.

Today had indeed not turned out as they had imagined. They had come close to losing their lives or killing Greg, as Danielle believed Trina would have killed him if Lori hadn't gotten to him first.

"He deserved to die!" Lori said, pulling away from Gabby. A steely look in her eyes sent a chill around the room. Gone was the quiet woman they all knew. A broken but strong woman was in her place who didn't regret her actions.

"How…?"

"He loves to brag. He told me when he came home what he had done, how he had killed Matt, but he couldn't find the photos. He was coming here today to search again. And I decided to follow him," Lori said. "Greg always thought I was foolish. He always thought I was stupid." She shook her head. "I don't know if I planned to kill him here or not. I don't know what I planned to do. All I know is I had to be here. If he found those photos, he would hold them against me for the rest of my life. I would never be free of him. He would never let me forget the mistake I made." She turned to Trina. "Where are the pictures? Which of you was he blackmailing?" Her eyes moved past Gwen and rested on Danielle. Her eyes softened. "You?"

With tears in her eyes, Danielle nodded. "I was young and stupid."

"So was I. I thought Frank cared for me. When I woke up, he had raped me, and he dropped me off in the middle of the night. He took away my innocence, and I haven't been the same since."

"I'm sorry that this happened to you ladies, but we need to get rid of the pictures and get out of here," Trina said while standing in front of the fireplace.

"We could burn them, since there's a fireplace," Danielle said.

"We don't have time! The police could be on their way right now, and I'm not letting Robert and Leah raise my child while I rot in prison. Let's go!" Gwen said while heading to the door.

"I'm making time, Gwen. Move, Trina."

Danielle tossed the photos into the fireplace, every one of them. Danielle was glad to see them go, with the red flames melting them into dust. Gone was her past. All that was left would be the memories.

"What are we going to do with the bodies?" Gabby asked.

The four women turned to the bodies; it was a gruesome sight. Danielle's stomach twisted. She had never seen a dead body before. She hadn't signed up for any of this—moving or getting rid of any bodies. Plus, Gwen needed to go to the restroom again, and she didn't want to leave any DNA in Matt's bathroom. It was time for the ladies to get out of there.

"You all should leave. I'll handle them," Lori said, emerging with an axe and garbage bags from the kitchen.

Danielle gulped. What on earth was the woman going to do with that?

"Pardon?" Gabby asked as the woman knelt in front of Matt's body.

She flashed them a look that made Danielle feel a chill. She didn't know if Lori had always been this way or if being married to Greg had loosened some nuts.

"I will deal with this mess. It's time for me to take back control," Lori said, just as she slammed the axe into Greg, separating the arm from the rest of his body.

"I'm out of here!" Gwen said, her hand over her mouth as she hurried out. Danielle followed, with no plans of witnessing more.

"What took you so long!" Gwen snapped as Trina got into the car. It had taken her an extra twenty minutes to join them.

"I was about to come back in," Danielle said, sounding worried.

Trina smiled. They probably thought crazy Lori had hacked her into pieces as well. "I had to clean the doorknobs and everything we touched. We can't leave any traces behind," Trina said as Lori walked out of the house.

"What's she doing? Why is she coming here?" Gwen asked, reaching for her gun.

They went quiet as she walked past them into the next hedge.

Trina noticed for the first time a black car, which Lori must have driven down in. They were still quiet as she walked past them again, carrying cleaning supplies in both hands. They all exchanged looks.

Trina gulped. Okay, she had underestimated the woman. When Trina emerged from cleaning upstairs, she had seen Lori hacking away while humming. She didn't even want to ponder if she was normal or insane. She was sure she had followed Greg with one thing in mind—to kill or be killed. He had pushed her to her limit, and she had snapped, fighting back. Only this time, fighting back meant killing her husband. She was like one of those women shown on TV who killed their husbands without remorse. But who was Trina to judge or wonder if she had premeditated his death? Greg had been an asshole who hurt his wife and thought the worst of women. He would have eventually killed Lori. And despite Trina having things under control, he could have hurt all of them.

"We should get out of here," Gwen said.

Trina agreed. The first half of the ride home was quiet until one of them started talking.

"This is crazy! So crazy!" Gabby said.

"What's going to happen now?" Danielle wondered.

"Well, you're free. Everything has been gotten rid of," Trina said. All the pictures had been destroyed, and no one else would be blackmailed again. Matt had been triggered when he saw Danielle and Lori at the shower, which had set his death in motion. Too bad he had messed with a vicious couple.

"What do you think is going to happen to Lori? She killed her husband," Danielle said.

The memory played in Trina's head. There has been so much rage as she shot him repeatedly. It had seemed like she had been waiting for that moment all her life.

"I don't know, but I feel Lori has a plan. She's not stupid like he thought," Trina said. Never underestimate anyone, especially the quiet ones. She looked submissive on the outside, but inside was a strong woman who had no qualms about cutting her husband into pieces like a butcher. She might just get away with it.

"Remember, we were never there," Gabby said.

"I don't even know you guys," Gwen said.

Trina laughed, and soon everyone was laughing. It was a relief, the tension easing. Today they'd had a close shave with death. The adrenaline. The fear. The blood. The thrill. Since she joined the tea party, Trina's life had indeed changed.

A lot was unsaid, but she guessed they were just too much in a daze with all that had happened. Perhaps later, when they were calm, they would talk about it.

"Thank you, guys, for doing this for me. I haven't said this, but I do appreciate you as friends. I don't think anyone I know would have gone to these lengths for me," Danielle said.

"We are always willing to help," Gabby said, hugging Danielle.

"Are you crying?" Trina asked with a smile as Gwen patted her eyes.

The woman glared at her. "Of course not! A bug flew into my eye. This cheap-ass car! Plus, where is my share of the money?"

Trina chuckled. Yeah, she had almost forgotten about the cash.

She had formed an unexplainable bond with the women. She had friends she had grown up with, and although she would be with them through thick and thin, there was just something about these women, and there was nothing she wouldn't do for them.

They got back to town early in the evening with enough hours before nightfall. They said their goodbyes and went to their cars. Trina returned the vehicle to the rental agency before heading home.

Trina took a long shower, marveling again at how the day had gone. Splendid, despite all that had happened. They had achieved results, and that was all that mattered.

She was pretty sure Lori would embrace her fate, whatever it was. That one was a tough cookie. A crazy, rich woman, she chuckled. Her husband had oppressed her for way too long, and she deserved the freedom that would follow, despite the cost, whatever it was.

When she emerged from the bathroom, she toweled her body, then slipped into a red dress with thin straps, which stopped right over her knees. The next thirty minutes were spent on her makeup.

Trina grabbed her coat and headed outside. She had a date to catch up with. And she was pretty sure with how excited she was; she would tear the clothes off Charles's body. Her mind settled on Lori for a second, but she shook it off. The woman had taken charge of her life. Trina was going to do the same as well.

ABOUT THE AUTHOR

Tina Luckett is a U.S. Army Veteran, adoring wife, loving mother of two adult daughters, and a long-time executive assistant. She's been writing for as long as she can remember but hadn't published her writing until recently.

Tina holds an Associate's Degree in Computer Science, a Bachelor's in Public Administration, and a Master's in Leadership. Now, she can add mother of two engineers to her resume.

When Tina isn't working, she enjoys spending as much time as possible with her family, friends and taking in the sights and events near her Michigan home.

For Tina, friendships aren't just something to collect. They're a way of life that has thoroughly enriched her own and others. And through her hard-earned wisdom, she's honored to offer her readers the same opportunities to find their happiness.

Connect with Tina
www.TinaLuckett.com
TinaLuckett7@gmail.com
IG: @Suite_Tea_Society
FB: @Lucketteer